The Dogs of War Series
Volume 8

The Sand Panthers

Also by Leo Kessler and available from
Spellmount Publishers in
The Dogs of War Series

THE
DOGS OF WAR SERIES
VOLUME 8

THE SAND PANTHERS

by

Leo Kessler

SPELLMOUNT

British Library Cataloguing in Publication Data:
A catalogue record for this book is available
from the British Library

Copyright © Charles Whiting 2006
Maps copyright © Charles Whiting 2006

ISBN 1-86227-335-9

First published in the UK in 1977.
Reprinted in 2006 by
Spellmount Limited
The Mill
Brimscombe Port
Stroud
Gloucestershire
GL5 2QG
UK

Tel: 0044 (0) 1453 883300
Fax: 0044 (0) 1453 883233
E-mail: enquiries@spellmount.com
Website: www.spellmount.com

1 3 5 7 9 8 6 4 2

The right of Charles Whiting to be identified
as the author of this work has been asserted by him
in accordance with the Copyright, Designs
and Patents Act 1988

THE SAND PANTHERS

SS Assault Regiment Wotan had been sent to join the Desert Rats, their objective to liberate the Egyptian army and to wrest the control of Alexandria from the British forces. But the men of Wotan found that Rommel didn't want them, and as they set off into the unmapped waste of the desert, they realised that something about this mission was wrong – very wrong indeed.

One thousand kilometres of uncharted desert lay before them: a blazing, barren, limitless hell, just sand and sun and sky – the only living creatures an enemy lying somewhere in wait for them, silent and unseen...

At that moment von Dodenburg had never felt gloomier in his life. His 1st Company had just suffered tremendous losses beating off the Tommy landing at Dieppe★ and now with the gaps in their ranks filled up with raw lads from the *Reich*, they were expected to go into action again – with Rommel in Africa.

'They don't like the SS out there, you know, Schulze,' von Dodenburg broke the heavy silence, disturbed only by the slither of the shingle on the beach below. 'All those sniff-noses of the *Afrikakorps* want to fight a private war with the Tommies, as if they were all fifteenth century knights in armour. They don't fancy the Black Guards' methods, I hear.'

'Maybe, sir,' Schulze commented, his lecherous blue eyes gleaming suddenly. 'But they've got those belly dancers out there, all bust and backside. Lovely grub! And sirs we'll get our knees brown!'

Von Dodenburg's gloom vanished. 'Of course, we'll get our knees brown!' he echoed excitedly.

As the first shrill silver notes of the bugle outside alerted the company, Major von Dodenburg cried:

'Africa, here we come!'

ASSAULT REGIMENT WOTAN WAS GOING TO WAR AGAIN!

> *Conversation between Major*
> *von Dodenburg and Sergeant-Major*
> *Schulze, 1 September, 1942*

★ See Kessler: *Forced March* for further details.

SECTION ONE:

PLAN OF ATTACK

'Now you are going to show those buck-
toothed Tommies back in the Delta how
really to put in a commando raid.'

Field-Marshal Rommel to Major von
Dodenburg, Tobruk, 1942

ONE

'Sie kommen!'

'Die Tommies?'

'Jawohl, Herr Generalfeldmarschall!'

The Desert Fox, Field-Marshal Erwin Rommel, swung round from the excited young Lieutenant of the *Afrikakorps*, who had just burst into the underground HQ with the news, and faced his staff. 'Gentlemen, the English commandos have begun their attack on Tobruk! Precisely on time as expected. The Tommies are very exact in their habits.'

There was a polite ripple of laughter among the bronzed-faced staff in their sweat-blackened khaki, which died with the sudden wail of an air-raid siren and the throaty crump of Tobruk flak.

The Desert Fox frowned. He looked at the Major with the Knight's Cross around his throat and the silver SS runes on his collar, but with the pale face and knees of a newcomer to the desert war 'Major von Dodenburg.'

'Field-Marshal?'

'Major, the English have been carrying out commando raids in the desert for two years now. And they have become very good at it. I should know: they nearly killed me last year. Fortunately we are in position to know exactly what their plans are – *in advance*,' he emphasised the words and paused, as if he expected the handsome SS Major to say something.

But the CO of the 1st Company of *Assault Regiment Wotan*, who had only arrived in Tobruk with his tanks the day before, remained silent.

He was new to the Desert and bewildered by the strange type of battle he had found himself plunged into so suddenly. Rommel nodded to Captain Schmidt, his bespectacled adjutant. 'The radio,' he barked.

The hot underground room was filled immediately with a confused babble of voices speaking in German and English, being transmitted to the HQ by the *Afrikakorps'* interceptor unit.

'The Tommy commandos are attacking in three groups,' Rommel explained. 'Two groups from the sea and one from the land. The aim of the land force is to establish a bridgehead to the south side of the harbour. When they have that, the other two forces will land from torpedo boats and motor launches. Together the three groups will remain within the Tobruk perimeter for twelve hours, wrecking our installations and destroying the bombproof oil tanks, which hold my reserve supplies of fuel.'

Major von Dodenburg's face must have reflected his disbelief at the accuracy of Rommel's outline of the enemy plan-of-attack, for the Desert Fox said: 'It is true to the very last detail, Major. Believe me, our sources of information in the enemy camp are unimpeachable.' He wiped the beads of sweat from his high forehead. 'That is the Tominies' plan. But, as you know, today is Friday 13 September – and it is going to be a very unlucky Friday the thirteenth indeed for the Tommies.'

The Field-Marshal's face hardened and von Dodenburg, puzzled by Wotan's sudden summons to the Middle East and by Rommel's personal attention to an officer of his low rank, could see why the Tommies called him the Desert Fox. There was something very sly about his ruthless, vulpine face. *'Today we are going to exterminate them, von Dodenburg!'*

* * *

It was dark but Colonel Haselden's SAS men and the German Jews, who, dressed in German uniform, had got them through the *Afrikakorps* perimeter without difficulty, knew exactly what to do They had trained long enough for this operation. Forming up into small teams, each with a German-speaking guide, they headed for the searchlights on the dock.

Colonel Haselden in the lead nodded his approval. Above them the twin-engined RAF Mitchells were zooming in, right on time, ignoring the flak which peppered the night sky all around them. At tree-top height they roared over the desert. Evil black eggs started to tumble from their bellies in lethal profusion. Haselden raised his voice above the racket of the exploding bombs. *'Come on, lads, let's give them hell!'* he cried.

Next to him, Sergeant Hayden raised his Tommy gun and fired a burst at the nearest searchlight. There was a scream of pain, a clatter of breaking glass and suddenly the silver finger of light poking the clouds vanished. A second later they surged forward to the attack.

Green and red Very lights, hissed into the sky. White tracer zipped through the air, and suddenly there was the angry snap and crackle of small arms fire everywhere. A commando went down, then another. A German Jew followed, cursing madly in German in his dying agony.

'Christ!' Haselden cried. 'Now the shit has really hit the fan!'

'You can say that again, sir,' Hayden gasped. 'You'd think the buggers'd known we were coming…' the high-pitched burst of Spandau fire nearly cut him in half. He tumbled to the ground, almost bringing the Colonel down.

'Are you hit bad, Hayden?' Haselden shouted.

'I've 'ad it, sir. Took half me sodding chest away,' Hayden slurred the words through a mouth which was rapidly filling with hot, salty blood. 'Fer chrissake, bugger off out of here…'

The words ended suddenly. Haselden peered down at Hayden's eyes, unnaturally large and startlingly terrified. His head lolled to one side just as the survivors of Force B's first wave went to ground, unable to advance against the withering German fire. In spite of the slugs hissing through the air like angry fire-flies, Haselden seemed unable to move. He was too dazed. Just as the first bullet slapped him a tremendous blow in the right shoulder and flung him against the wall of the nearest hut, he knew that the operation was already a failure. The Germans had known they were coming. As he started to slither down the wall, dragging a bright red trail of blood behind him, the dying Colonel realized with a sense of overwhelming bitterness that they had been betrayed!

★ ★ ★

For a moment the loudspeaker in the claustrophobic staff room fell silent. Von Dodenburg started to wipe the pearls of sweat from his face. The loudspeaker crackled into life again and von Dodenburg's hand remained where it was. That horrible, pain-racked voice of the dying British naval officer, trapped in the sinking torpedo boat filled with dead sailors and soldiers, came through again.

It was breathless with hysteria. *'Oh Christ, I can't stand it… My foot's fallen off… Where's my bloody foot?'*

Von Dodenburg felt the hairs at the back of his neck stand erect and he shuddered in spite of himself.

There was a pause, broken only by the dying man's harsh breathing. Then he sobbed, *'They're all dead…. All dead…. They've left me. My God…'*

Over the loudspeaker came the most unnerving sound of all. The wailing, uncontrolled sobs of a man breaking down altogether. Rommel nodded to his adjutant. Schmidt reached up and clicked off the loud speaker. Outside the sound of firing was dying away. Inside the underground HQ, the staff officers stood there transfixed, horrified by the slaughter of the British force although they were all hardened veterans who had undergone the mayhem of the trenches in the First World War.

Rommel remained unmoved. His face was set in a smile of ruthless triumph. The Desert Fox had beaten the British again and he was unable to conceal his sense of delight. Suddenly he brought his fly-swat down on the map table with a smart crack. The staff officers jumped, startled.

'Meine Herren,' he announced. 'Those who are left of the Tommies are running now into the desert for their lives. We have beaten them decisively!'

There was a murmur of agreement from the assembled officers. Rommel slapped his fly-swatter down on the table once again.

'Gentlemen, what you have just experienced is already history, and we'll leave the Tommies to reflect upon the past – they are very good at it. We Germans have other and better things to do.'

He turned and stared at von Dodenburg, as if trying to see something behind the young officer's face. 'So, Major, you have seen your first desert commando raid.' The Field-Marshal thrust out his pugnacious, obstinate chin aggressively. 'Now *you* are going to show those buck Tommies back in the Delta how really to put in a commando raid.' He pulled on his peaked *Afrikakorps* cap and nodded to Schmidt. 'Attend me at zero hundred hours tomorrow morning, von Dodenburg. I have work for your SS ruffians. *Gute Nacht, meine Herren.*' Casually touching his fly-swatter to his cap, the man who had beaten every British general in Africa for the last two years, went out into the blazing Libyan night.

TWO

Major von Dodenburg shivered and dug his chin deeper into the collar of his greatcoat. In the weeks to come he would always associate the stink of gasoline on the cold African dawn with the desert.

He turned and stared at the sand waste beyond Tobruk's perimeter. Behind him Field-Marshal Rommel was hurrying from his command halftrack to his portable thunderbox. As always before a crisis, the Swabian General's stomach was upset. Two soldiers stood by, shovels over their shoulders, at the ready.

The scene of the night's attack was strewn with wrecked British equipment: Rifles, machine-guns, bits of paper, uniform, used cartridge cases – and dead men, sprawled in grotesque postures. Further on, the vehicles, which had brought the Toni Commandos to the perimeter wire, were still burning, sending up pails of thick smoke into the overcast dawn sky. Von Dodenburg shivered again. It was a sombre sight.

He adjusted his collar and doubled over to the command halftrack, its many radios already humming and crackling with the business of a new day at war. He snapped smartly to attention in front of the waiting Field-Marshal. *'Hauptsturmführer von Dodenburg zur Stelle, Herr General-Feldmarschall!'* he reported, staring at the distant horizon behind the Desert Fox's right shoulder, and realizing to his horror that Sergeant- Major Schulze and his crony Corporal Matz were busily looting from the back of the Field-Marshal's supply truck the British rations which his own staff had looted from the dead Commandos one hour earlier. 'That damned Schulze,' he told himself hotly, 'I'll have the nuts off him for this!' Then he breathed a quick prayer that the two looters would get away with it without being discovered. The SS were not exactly popular with Rommel's staff as it was.

'Morning von Dodenburg,' Rommel said easily, although his broad face was drawn and grey from the new bout of his stomach complaint. He flicked his fly swatter casually to his peaked cap. 'I suppose you are wondering why I have had you and your armour posted to Africa away from the fleshpots of France?'

'One doesn't wonder – at least out loud – about the reasons for a Field-Marshal's actions, Sir,' von Dodenburg replied.

Rommel's tight mouth relaxed into a little smile. 'Typical SS, von Dodenburg. You are never ones to be impressed by rank. All right, you saw what happened last night on the perimeter, and the Tommies might have pulled it off – the operation was well planned *for them* – if it had not been for our friends in Alexandria and Cairo.'

'Friends, sir?' von Dodenburg ventured and breathed an inner sigh of relief. Schulze, a huge sack of looted British goods over his massive shoulder, was stealing back to the Wotan lines followed by Matz, similarly laden.

'Yes. The Egyptians are sick of the Tommies. At least the intellectuals and most of the younger officers are. They want to be rid of the English. So far all they have done has been to supply us with information about the movements of the Eighth Army. Hence last night. But now the Delta is almost wide-open for us, they are prepared to go a stage further.' The Desert Fox sighed like a man who has just too many burdens to bear. 'However, like our dear Italian allies, the Egyptians are not the bravest of the brave. They need – how shall I put it? – a little backbone.' The full rage of his frustration broke through and he snorted, 'Spaghetti-eaters and niggers, what a pathetic bunch of allies we have!'

Von Dodenburg did not rise to the outburst. Beyond the command halftrack the Arab grave-diggers under the command of German NCOs were swarming out into the desert to collect and bury the British dead; the Field-Marshal was always very correct about the

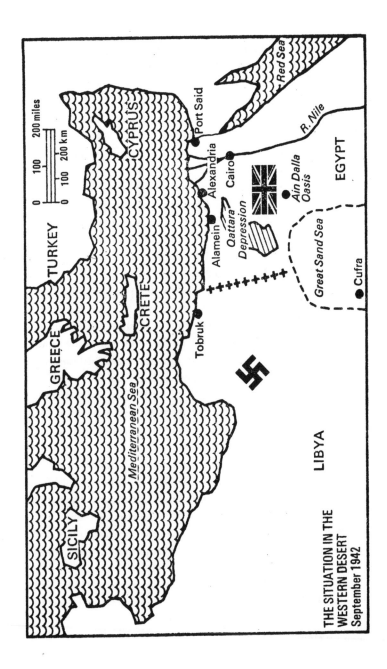

THE SITUATION IN THE
WESTERN DESERT
September 1942

dead. After he had photographed them for his scrapbook, he always insisted that they should be buried, whatever the circumstances.

'Well, von Dodenburg, as I say they need backbone – and now I'm prepared to give them just that.' He took his fly-swatter and drew a straight line in the sand. 'The Tommy positions ahead of us to the East, stretching from the Mediterranean to the Qattara Depression. Just as I would do, the Tommy generals have positioned their forces with an unturnable flank to their right – the sea – and another on to their left – the salt sea of the Qattara Depression, which is totally unsuitable for heavy vehicles. Clear, von Dodenburg?'

'Clear, sir,' the SS Major answered smartly, the little snake of apprehension already beginning to uncoil itself in his brain.

'Now those commandos last night came into our positions through the back door into Libya – here.'

Rommel drew a wavy line far below the spot where the Qattara Depression would be. 'Starting from the Mustafa Barracks in Alexandria, the Tommies drive south west until they reach Ain Dalla Oasis. There, according to our Egyptian informants, the Tommy commandos plunge into the Great Sand Sea.' He tapped the second line. 'About here. It is a large sloping wall of sand which runs up a summit of rock. Again according to the niggers, the ascent is not easy, but it can be done, as we saw last night. Once that ascent is taken, there is nearly 800 kilometres of almost uncharted desert to cross. But the Tommies manage to cross it regularly.'

Von Dodenberg intervened – 'But the Tommies do not use tracked vehicles, Field-Marshal!' The Desert Fox beamed at him, as if he were a schoolmaster pleased with a particularly bright pupil. *'Ach, mein lieber von Dodenburg*, you have seen through me?'

'If you mean, sir, you have a plan to send my Wotan through the desert into Egypt, yes I have. But to what purpose, if I may ask?'

'Well, von Dodenburg, I have just said that those niggers in the Delta need some backbone before they do anything.' He licked his cracked lips, and stared directly at von Dodenburg's pale, hard face. 'Major, you and your Wotan are going to be the ones who give them that backbone. Now listen…'

THREE

'*Muck 'em all,*
Muck 'em all, The long and the short and the tall
You'll get no promotion this side of the ocean
So cheer up my lads, muck'em—'
'*Shut your cakehole, or I'll have yer on a fizzer, you idle man!*'

The raucous North Country voice died immediately at the roar of some angry NCO from within Alexandria's gleaming white Mustafa Barracks. At the gate the skinny little Arab with a bold hook of a nose jumped visibly and clutched at his skinny-ribbed donkey's rein.

The regimental policeman – all gleaming brass, brilliant white-blancoed equipment, sparkling boots and crisp starched khaki – raised his swagger cane and snarled out of the side of his mouth. 'Sod off you dirty Gippo wog – and get that poxy nag out of here before he pisses in front of the guardroom!' The little Egyptian peddlar was unafraid. Indeed he moved closer to this lance-corporal on guard and held up the pictures he had concealed in his skinny brown claw.

The sentry gasped and took in the first picture: dark skinned, middle-aged woman with a twenties hairdo doing something he had thought impossible with a yellow-toothed donkey. 'You dirty Gippo-wog bugger!' he exclaimed, not taking his eyes off the photos. 'That's all you filthy lot think on – dipping yer wick and half inching our rations.' He waved his swagger cane at the grinning peddlar, his face crimson with righteous indignation. 'Now be off with you, or I'll have you inside the nick in double-quick time!'

The Egyptian shot a furtive look to both sides. Urgently he whispered out of the corner of his mouth in perfect Upper Class English. 'That's exactly what I want you to do, Corporal.' The MP's mouth dropped open stupidly. 'What did you say?'

'You heard me, man! Get me inside and make it look as if you are arresting me for loitering. I must see Brigadier Young at once – and they have spies everywhere. Now move!'

The sentry moved! Next instant a wailing, protesting peddlar was dragged into the barracks by the scruff of his skinny neck, leaving his loudly braying donkey behind him. Major Slaughter had done it again.

★ ★ ★

'Well, Slaughter?' Brigadier Young barked. Above him the mechanical fan barely stirred the stiflingly hot air.

'A total failure,' Slaughter answered, removing his disguise. 'The Jerries knew Haselden was coming. They wiped the floor with our poor chaps. I doubt if we'll get a dozen of them back through the Sand Sea in the end.'

'Treachery?' Young, a white-haired, red-faced officer with a trim Regular Army moustache queried.

Slaughter nodded slowly.

'By whom – our people?' the Brigadier rapped, leaning forward in anticipation.

Slaughter took his time. Outside a harsh military voice was barking: *'Now swing them arms there! … Bags of swank! … and open them legs, you bunch of pregnant penguins – nothing will fall out, you know!'*
'No sir. It was the Gippos. That crowd around Nasser and the rest of those young Gippo officers. They'll go to any length to get us out of Egypt.' Young bit his bottom lip.

'They've got their eyes and ears everywhere. When our chaps from the SAS or the LRDG[1] prepare to move out into the blue, there are Gippo mess waiters, the sanitary wallahs, the Gippo hawkers, all taking note of our every move and passing it on to the Nasser crowd.'

Long-Range Desert Group.

'It's damnable!' Brigadier Young exploded, his face flushing angrily. 'Why the devil don't we sling the whole greasy bunch of them inside, once and for all? Skulking around here in the base area and betraying all those good men up there in the desert.'

Slaughter shook his head slowly. 'Afraid no-can-do, sir. Then we'd really set the cat among the pigeons. Even the Fat Boy' – he meant the grossly overweight Egyptian king – 'would have to forget about his whores and come out on the side of the young officers. We'd have the whole of the Delta up in arms and at the moment with this new chap General Montgomery preparing a fresh offensive up the blue, we can't afford that kind of thing, sir.'

Young sighed and looked up at the flaking white ceiling, as if seeking solace up there. 'I suppose you're right, Slaughter. You always are.'

'Mostly, sir,' Slaughter replied without a trace of irony. For eighteen years he had been in the political intelligence section of the Cairo High Commissioner's office and he had lost his English sense of humour – if he had ever possessed one. In nearly two decade in Egypt, mixing with the Egyptians and the desert Arabs for months on end without ever speaking to another Englishman, he had adopted many Egyptian mannerisms, including taking everything completely seriously. 'Once we have beaten the Hun in the desert and the Delta is no longer threatened, then the High Commissioner will act. He'll put the lot of them behind bars where they belong. But at the moment, everything is on a knife edge. Only last week, the Fat Boy had the audacity to tell Lampson[2] "When the war's over, then for God's sake put down the white man's burden – and go".'

'I understand, Slaughter. All right, what can we do? I presume you are here for a reason.'

'I am, sir.' Slaughter hesitated a fraction of a second, as if he were finding it a little difficult to formulate what he had to say next. 'Assuming, sir, that the situation in the Delta is on a knife edge, with Gippos ready to have a crack, at us any day now, what do you think it would take for them to make a move?'

---

2. The British Minister to Cairo.

Young laughed coarsely. 'A bloody miracle, Slaughter!' he exclaimed. 'You know better than I do what a bunch of cowards they are. When your back's turned, all right, they might risk sticking a knife in it, but if you turn and face them–' he shrugged. 'They're off with their tails between their skinny legs.'

'Agreed, sir. But in this case I think we've got our backs to them. The troops are pretty thin on the ground down here with Montgomery preparing for his offensive in the desert, and – with all respect – I don't think the staff wallahs at GHQ, Cairo would frighten them if it came to trouble.

'Now, sir,' Slaughter went on, 'what if the Gippos receive a stiffening of Germans?'

'Huns? But who and how?'

'I don't know about the "who" sir, but the "how" is not too difficult. *Through the Sand Sea!*'

Young looked at him aghast. 'But they've never tried it before,' he stuttered. 'I mean...'

Slaughter looked at him coldly. 'I've good reason to believe that Rommel is planning something of that sort, sir.'

'How do you mean, Slaughter?'

The English agent lowered his brown eyes almost demurely. 'My boys, of course, sir.'

'Of course,' Young echoed, grateful to Slaughter that he did not have to look him in the eye at that particular moment. The Major had been in Egypt too long. He had taken up too many of the Wog vices, including that one. 'But if your boys are correct in their estimate, what can we do? All I could give you to cover the exits from the Sand Sea is what is left of the SAS and LRDG.' He shrugged. 'Perhaps a couple of score men at the most.'

'I'll take them, sir – with thanks,' Slaughter said hastily. 'But I want more – I want the Horsemen of St George, lots of them.'

'Horsemen of St George?' the Brigadier queried. Slaughter laughed coldly. 'That is what the desert Arabs call golden sovereigns. Sir, I want to call out the tribes. For every German they capture, I'll promise them twenty Horsemen. It's a small fortune for them.'

The Brigadier shuddered in spite of the heat. 'Call out the tribes,' he exclaimed. 'My God, you know what the desert Arabs do to a white man!'

'I do! But it's either that or the Germans will get through into the Delta.'

The Brigadier sighed, and ringing the little bell on his desk, said, 'You know, Slaughter, you've been too long in this damned country. It has corrupted you.'

Slaughter's dark brown eyes gleamed momentarily. 'I expect it has, sir,' he said calmly enough. 'Now do I get the Horsemen of St George?'

'You do, Slaughter, you do…'

* * *

Five minutes later an observer of the entrance to Alexandria's Mustafa Barracks would have been treated to the sight of a burly sergeant-major sending a skinny little wog flying out of the gate, propelled by the gleaming toe of the NCO's size eleven ammunition boot.

The little wog glared malevolently up at him from the dust, but he said and did nothing, until the NCO had turned and stamped back into the barracks. Then he struggled to his feet, hawked, and spat defiantly onto the baking ground. Limping badly he struggled back to his waiting donkey. With a grunt he slung his new burden over its back. The pathetic creature brayed in protest. The wog dug his nail-tipped goad into its hide and it moved forward, back into the desert, bearing with it the exact price of two hundred dead Germans.

FOUR

Sergeant-Major Schulze, Assault Regiment Wotan's senior NCO, cursed and thrust his peaked cap to the back of his shaven head, 'What's this? The feeding of the bloody five thousand?'

He stared across at the hundreds of men milling around the soup kettles, waiting for their breakfast, while cooks, stripped to the waist, the sweat running off their naked arms into the food, tried to feed them. 'How can I be expected to grub up my guts with that mob rushing the goulash cannon, eh?'

Corporal Matz, Schulze's crony, glanced up at the big blond ex-docker, a look of contempt on his wrinkled, leathery face. 'You are the senior NCO in the senior regiment of the senior division of the SS, ain't yer?'

'Agreed, my horrible little wet dream,' Schulze said.

'Then what are you standing there for – like a big fart in a trance? You go automatically to the head of the queue. It's your right. After all, we are the Wotan, you know.' Matz jingled his mess tins in anticipation. 'Well, what are we waiting for? Come on!'

Brutally the two SS noncoms pushed their way through the disgruntled *Afrikakorps* men, crying 'Make way for a naval officer!' Here and there a soldier turned and began to protest, but their angry comments died on their cracked lips when they saw the black and white armbands of the Armed SS on the two NCOs' sleeves. Not even the veterans of Rommel's *Afrikakorps* wanted to tangle with the SS.

The first cook looked up at them dully. 'First canteen – nigger sweat; second – rations.' Schulze accepted the steaming black ersatz coffee in his first canteen and soup in the other. Together he and Matz pushed their way through the sullen crowd and walked across the desert to a halftrack, its bogies almost half buried in drifting sand, a little outpost of blackness in that gleaming white. It offered shade, but no coolness.

With a sigh, Schulze and Matz dropped to the burning ground. Schulze put down his canteens and pulled out a can of the British beer he had looted from Rommel's supply truck the previous day. Taking his bayonet, he punched a hole in it, thrusting the can to his lips swiftly before the warm beer had a chance to spurt out.

He took a few sips, then he dropped the can in disgust. 'Bloody sand – it's half full of sand,' he snarled. 'This desert! God knows why the *Führer* wants it! There's sand in the food; sand in the coffee; fucking sand in everything. If there was any nooky in this damned desert, I wouldn't be surprised if there was sand up there, as well!'

'There ain't, yer know,' Matz said, greedily finishing the last of his soup.

'Ain't what, you asparagus Tarzan?' Schulze asked morosely.

'Sand up there,' Matz replied easily. Schulze's bottom lip trembled. 'You mean…you mean,' he breathed in awe, 'that…that there's *that* here?'

Matz finished the last of the soup with a flourish and wiped his mouth with the back of his sleeve. 'What?'

'Tail, pussy, nooky, something to snake.' He grabbed Matz's jacket and pulled the little corporal to him eagerly. '*THAT!*'

'Oh, that,' Matz said casually. 'Course there is.' Schulze released his hold and breathed out hard, a sudden gleam in his eyes. He crooked his big forefinger at Matz and said: 'Give!'

'Down by the Quay near the cranes.'

'And you mean you didn't tell your old pal, Matzi!'

'*Officers only*,' Matz answered and finished the last of the beer.

'Officers,' Schulze barked contemptuously, 'I've shat 'em!' His blue eyes sparkled. 'All that good Tommy bully beef yesterday really put me on. It put so much lead in my pencil, I don't know who to write to first!'

'Whores from spaghetti-land. Last month the Tommies dropped a bomb on the place and that little garden dwarf of a king of theirs awarded the ones wounded a medal for bravery. Our officers who were killed were listed as K.I.A.[1]'

'What a way to go – knocked off on the job!' The big Sergeant-Major rose hastily to his feet. 'Well,' he demanded, 'what are you sitting there for, growing corns on your ass. Let's go. I'm limping already, just thinking about it…'

* * *

Von Dodenburg, smoking his post-breakfast cigar, smiled and watched the two NCOs plodding away through the thick sand to the coast, telling himself that it would take all their celebrated ingenuity to get them into the brothel, which was reserved for 'golden pheasants' and staff officers over the rank of major. Then he dismissed the two NCOs from his thoughts, and grinding out the cigar, walked to the operations tent for his first meeting of the day.

Captain Professor Dr Hans Reichert was already waiting for him inside. The elderly Captain who rose to salute von Dodenburg seemed as cool as a spring day despite the intense heat. There was not a trace of perspiration on his face. 'The man must have ice-water in his veins,' von Dodenburg told himself a little angrily as he motioned the Captain to a seat.

'I've been told by Field-Marshal Rommel that you will brief me on the difficulties of the operation, Captain…er…Professor Reichert?' he said.

Reichert, who had once been the University of Heidelberg's leading Egyptologist, cleared his throat importantly, as if he were now about to deliver a lecture. 'That is so, I believe, Major.'

'I know, Reichert,' von Dodenburg snapped, irritated by the heat and the man's academic manner. All the same he knew that he had

---

1. Killed-in-Action.

spent half a lifetime in the desert and was the *Afrikakorps'* foremost expert on it. He needed his assistance badly. 'Now this is the problem. I have been ordered to take my Mark IV tanks and my halftracks through the Sand Sea into Egypt. Ten tanks, ten halftracks and 150 men. Now what am I going to be faced with?'

Again the ex-Professor cleared his throat. 'There are many problems,' he said carefully. 'Very many.'

'All right, tell me them,' von Dodenburg snapped. 'Come on get on with it!'

Reichert's face flushed like that of a maiden lady who had just felt a man's hand thrust up her skirt. 'There is the question of navigation for example,' he began. 'The Sand Sea is featureless – rather like the Luneburg Heath with no outcrops of rock. You'll have to use the sun compass.'

'Sun compass?' von Dodenburg questioned.

'It is a very simple way of navigating. It depends upon knowing the exact sun time. From this we can determine the sun's bearing throughout the day. I have personally always found it easier to remember that at midday, when the sun is due south, the shadow falls due north. Hence the direction of movement at right angles to the shadow will obviously be either due east or west. Once one has absorbed that fact, one needs only to note the distance one has travelled to determine to within a few hundred metres one's position in relation to the starting point. Is that clear, Major?'

Reichert did not wait for the Major's response, but carried on as if he had reached a particularly important point in one of his *Hauptseminars* and did not want to be stopped by some foolish question. 'Then there is the problem of driving. Once the sand has dried after dawn, one finds that each vehicle is followed by a huge plume of sand which not only gives one's position away for kilometres, but also–'

Major von Dodenburg held up his hand. 'Hold it, hold it, Professor!' he commanded. 'Let me ask you one question – and one question only. Do you think we can make it?'

'From Cufra, our last outpost in the desert, you will have to cover virtually one thousand kilometres of uncharted desert with one hundred and fifty men who are not yet acclimatized, plus twenty heavy vehicles which will eat up tremendous amounts of fuel and water – where there is not one solitary well.' Reichert paused and stared up at the young officer. 'With luck, you'll make it, Major,' he concluded.

'Excellent,' von Dodenburg exclaimed. 'And I am especially glad. For your sake, Professor.'

'My sake?'

'Yes, my dear sir.' Major von Dodenburg grinned at the other man's sudden bewilderment. 'Because you are coming with us, as our guide and mentor.'

'Oh, my goodness!' Professor Dr Hans Reichert slumped weakly in his chair. 'Oh my goodness me!'

Von Dodenburg rose to his feet and reached for his cap. 'All right then, Prof,' he snapped, 'let's get our fingers out. We've got a lot to do today.' Briskly he strode out into the desert's sun burning white brilliance. Wotan had exactly forty-eight hours left before it moved out.

FIVE

The next forty-eight hours flew by. There were a hundred and one problems for von Dodenburg to solve. In the oven-hot air, the half-naked Wotan men sweated over the vehicles, preparing them for the long trek into the unknown desert. The blond Major, his face already burnt a brick-red by the sun, was here, there and everywhere, knowing that to relax for an instant would be fatal.

He strode from crew to crew, checking them and their vehicles and coming to loathe the burning-red ball of the sun, which beat down upon them so relentlessly. He thought longingly of the cool French coast which they had just left for these burnished sands and stifling opaque haze, which shimmered blindingly.

On the first day, von Dodenburg, Schulze, and Captain Reichert concentrated on checking that the tanks and halftracks were correctly fuelled up and armed. Forcing himself to walk slowly, von Dodenburg inspected the outside of each vehicle in that stifling heat, and then clambered inside the red-hot metal boxes to check the mass of dials, the speedometer, the revolution counter, the pressure gauges, the cannon-firing mechanism.

On the morning of the second day he took his own command vehicle for a hard ride into the desert, accompanied by Schulze and the 'Prof', with Matz at the wheel. Within two hours, each man was reduced to the state of a wet rag. Time and time again the metal pins joining the track-plates broke on the hard, stony ground of the desert, leaving them with the back breaking task of hammering in another.

At midday von Dodenburg began to call on his fellow COs of the armoured regiments all around, whose Mark IIIs and Mark IVs were equipped with specially hardened link-pins, designed specifically for the desert. But none of them had pins to spare for Assault Regiment Wotan. Fuming with rage, von Dodenburg cried to Reichert, 'You would think we were the bloody enemy – and not the Tommies, goddamit!'

Reichert allowed himself a faint smirk, 'But, if I may be forgiven for saying so my dear Major, you are.'

Von Dodenburg spun round on him. 'What the hell is that supposed to mean, eh?'

The look of naked fury in his eyes wiped the smirk off the Professor's face. 'I meant that the gentlemen of the *Afrikakorps* think you of the SS are lowering the tone of the war in the desert. As they see it, the sooner the SS vanishes into the desert – *for good* – the better everything will be.'

Von Dodenburg slumped weakly against the burning canvas of the HQ tent. 'Oh, my back,' he croaked. 'What a bloody war!' Wearily he wiped the sweat off his dripping brow, only to feel the second wave of perspiration swamp his forehead the very next moment. 'What in hell's name am I going to do? By Christ, I'll go right to the Field-Marshal about this!'

'With respect, Major, the gentlemen of the Staff would probably never let you get within sniffing distance of His Excellency.'

Von Dodenburg slammed his clenched fist on the table violently. 'I must have those pins!' he cried.

'Sir.' It was Schulze, who had been standing at the flap of the tent all the time.

'Yes, what is it?'

'Sir, I think me and Matzi might be able to get those pins for you,' he ventured with unusual hesitancy.

'But how?' the Major cried. 'Come on, don't stand around like a spare prick at a wedding. Out with it!'

'Well, sir, perhaps you remember yesterday morning, me and Matzi went of down to the Quay – to look for supplies.'

'You mean – *whores*,' von Dodenberg sneered. Schulze stared down at his big dusty boots. 'I suppose you might put it like that, sir,' he said. 'Well, sir, me and Matzi found out we weren't particularly welcome at the house, sir. It seems it's only meant for senior officers of the staff. But we thought we'd come a long way to get inside them pearly gates and it was going to be a long time before we'd be able to rip off another piece, so we had a bit of a think and we came up with this.' He reached inside his trouser pocket and brought out a pair of epaulettes, heavy with the gilt of a full colonel.

'You mean you put these on your shoulders and passed yourselves off as officers!' von Dodenburg gasped.

'In the *Afrikakorps*, they could shoot you for that,' the Professor exclaimed.

'But I can't see what your obscene pleasures and obvious infringement of military law have got to do with my link-pins, Schulze?' von Dodenburg interjected.

A look of both embarrassment and wicked amusement appeared in the big Hamburger's blue eyes. 'Well, sir, the macaroni-eater took a fancy to us. She said we could have seconds – for nothing. But we'd have to wait till her next customer, Colonel Hartmann, had completed his daily session of mattress gymnastics.'

'You mean Colonel Hartmann – *of Supply*?' von Dodenburg cried incredulously.

'The same, sir,' Schulze answered and looked down modestly. 'Every day, on the stroke of twelve, he's in there for two solid hours. He's a bit long in the tooth, sir, and it takes him a while to raise – er – a smile.'

'Schulze, I'm ten kilometres ahead of you, speeding at a hundred an hour. Correct me, if I'm wrong. But you're going to break military law yet again by assuming a false rank and while Colonel Hartmann is enjoying his luncheon break, you are going to borrow his vehicle, proceed to his HQ and do a little impromptu requisitioning. Right?'

Schulze beamed down at him. 'Right, sir!'

'Then what are you standing there for, you great oaf – *get on with it*! It's already thirteen hundred hours. You've only got sixty minutes left.'

'*Sir!*' Schulze flew through the door.

Professor Reichert slumped back in his chair. '*Ache du lieber Himmel!*' he sighed weakly. 'The methods of the Armed SS! My God what have I got myself into now?'

'What indeed?' von Dodenburg grinned at him, happy for the first time that day.

SIX

Two o'clock came and went and there was still no sign of Schulze and Matz. Half past two arrived and von Dodenburg surveying the distance between their camp and the quay through his binoculars, still could not make them out. Three o'clock struck and he was beginning to worry that for once, the two rogues had really run into serious trouble.

Thirty minutes later, a great plume of sand, thrown up by several vehicles hurrying towards Wotan at great speed made von Dodenburg's heart leap excitedly; Schulze and Matze had pulled it off!

But he was mistaken. The man who got out of the leading halftrack was none other than Field-Marshal Rommel himself. He pushed back his sand goggles, saluted the SS men standing rigidly to attention in the burning sun, and took von Dodenburg by the arm with a curt: 'We shall go for a little walk, Major.'

Anticipating the worst, von Dodenburg allowed himself to be guided into the desert, watched by the curious eyes of his own men and those of Rommel's staff.

But Schulze and Matz had not been found out. Rommel's first words indicated that he had come to Wotan's HQ on a completely different matter.

'Walls, you know, my dear Major, do have ears – although we have very few of them in the desert,' Rommel began and stopped, obviously confident that he was out of earshot. 'Von Dodenburg, I have come up to give you your final instructions and I would suggest you keep them to yourself and don't reveal them to that old fart of a schoolmaster you've picked as your adviser.'

Von Dodenburg grinned at the Desert Fox's description of Professor Reichert. 'I understand, sir,' he said.

'Good.' Rommel swung his whisk at an importuning fly. 'My Intelligence section has information that the Tommies are pushing out a wide screen of light tanks and armoured cars to the front of their positons at El Alamein. Obviously that new general of theirs is planning something. I want you to avoid that screen. If you do chance to bump into it, destroy it completely; prisoners will not be taken! You understand? I want no word of your operation to get back to the British HQ. Clear?'

'Clear, sir.'

'Two.' Rommel ticked off the points on his fingers. 'There will be no turning back. Once the Tommy patrols out there in the Sand Sea discover your tracks, they will attempt to block the route and I might well need it again. Understand this, you either make it, or you don't come back at all.' Rommel looked hard at the younger man and von Dodenburg realized that the 'Prof' was right; the gentlemen of the *Afrikakorps* did hate the SS, Rommel had just issued a virtual sentence of death.

'Three. Once you are through the Sand Sea—'

'*If*,' a cynical little voice at the back of von Dodenburg's head interrupted.

'And down the Ascent, I want you to make at full speed for the Ain Dalla Oasis, which is held by the Egyptian Army and a handful of Tommies who are there to watch them. There you will meet your contact.'

Von Dodenburg looked at the Desert Fox's ruthless face. 'But who is my contact, sir?' he asked a little helplessly, raising the point which had puzzled him ever since the mission had been proposed.

'Don't worry about that. You will be contacted all right, once you are there. Never fear. He —' suddenly Rommel burst out in a guffaw of coarse laughter — 'he will see to that.'

He thrust out his hand. 'Major, from now on it's march or croak!' he rapped.

'March or croak, sir!'

Rommel grinned. Von Dodenburg grinned. They understood each other: the young Major and the middle-aged Field-Marshal, who would kill himself at the *Führer's* order, within two years.

Five minutes later, he was gone. Von Dodenburg would never see him again.

* * *

It was five o'clock when the big halftrack, flying a full colonel's flag on its bonnet, rolled into the camp, followed by a captured British 3-ton truck laden up to the roof with link-pins, and manned by a half-a-dozen grinning Italians. Matz at the wheel drew up with a flourish and tipped Schulze, who was standing upright with a pair of black lace drawers wrapped around his head, neatly over the open windscreen onto the sand directly in front of von Dodenburg.

The young Major looked down at him and groaned, 'Oh God! As pissed as a rat!'

Schulze grinned and struggled to his feet. Swaying wildly, he flung his CO a magnificent salute – and missed his forehead completely. 'Sir, my tonsils is floating in chianti and Tommy whisky.'

Von Dodenburg glanced at the grinning Italians and realized they were drunk too. 'Matz,' he barked at the little corporal, who looked sober. 'What the devil have you rogues been up to?'

'Better not ask, sir,' he said darkly. 'All I can say is we've got what you wanted, we've adopted half the spaghetti-eaters' Army,' he indicated the drunken Italian soldiers, 'and this.' He pulled back what looked like a silken bed-spread which covered the rear end of the halftrack to reveal bottle after bottle of champagne, cases of cigars and a pile of what appeared to be frilly female underwear.

Von Dodenburg's mouth dropped open in dismay. 'Where did you get that?'

'All I can say, sir,' Matz replied ponderously, 'is this. That house down on the quay will never be the same again, Colonel Hartmann has suffered an unfortunate accident which will keep him on his back for several months, I'm afraid – and…' He hesitated.

'And what?' Von Dodenburg demanded.

'I think we'll have about till dawn before the head hunters[1] come looking for us…'

---

1. Military policemen.

SECTION TWO:

INTO THE GREAT SAND SEA

'Two thousand years later, Major von Dodenburg, they are still out here, having in the meantime become more vicious and stranger in their ways.'

Professor Reichert to von Dodenburg in the Great Sand Sea

ONE

Von Dodenburg was already awake. Through the open flap of his tent, he could see the sky paling imperceptibly so that the desert all around took on a series of different hues.

For a moment he lay there in the warm, comforting sleeping bag casting his mind over the many problems ahead and wondering whether he had forgotten anything, made a mistake anywhere. He knew from the 'Prof' that a false estimate of the amount of water they might need to cross the Sand Sea, even a mistake in the number of salt tablets, so vital in that intense heat, could spell disaster.

Finally he decided it was too late to worry now, and with a groan rose from his sleeping bag. The new day had begun.

The next hour passed swiftly. While von Dodenburg strode from vehicle to vehicle, checking that everyone would be prepared to move out on the signal, the crews prepared their breakfast, for there would be no more cooking until they were well out into no-man's land and away from prying British eyes.

Briefly von Dodenburg exchanged a few words with a very pale Schulze, who had his head wrapped in a rag soaked in vinegar and spoke in an unusually soft voice, as if he were afraid that any loud noise might shatter his skull for good. The major tapped him slightly on the shoulder and said in commiseration: 'If you feel like you look, you big rogue, you must be feeling rotten. All the same thank you for those links. The crews worked all night hammering the new ones in.'

At precisely 0630 hours, 14 October, 1942, 1st Company SS Assault Regiment Wotan started to move out. Standing on the turret of his command tank, next to a morose Schulze, and the 'Prof', von Dodenburg watched his force begin their advance into the desert.

The clatter of the tank tracks, the rattle of the towed 088mm guns, the thump of the halftracks bouncing over the rough ground were the only sounds to be heard. The men's cries and shouts had died immediately in the cloud of dust raised by the departing vehicles. Now the troopers, standing in the turrets and on the decks of the halftracks, had their sand goggles down and their scarves pulled up over their mouths to keep out the choking dust. Von Dodenburg surveyed the young faces of his men. They looked worried at the prospect of the long journey into the unknown that lay before them, but not afraid.

The 'Prof' seemed to read the Major's thoughts, for he said: 'They won't let you down, Major.'

'Lot of aspagarus Tarzans – still got the eggshell behind their spoons,' Schulze growled grumpily.

Von Dodenburg touched his throat mike. 'All right, Matz – roll 'em!' he commanded.

Matz let out the clutch. The 25-ton metal monster lurched forward. They were on their way.

★ ★ ★

Wotan moved in a long column with the 'Prof' in von Dodenburg's lead tank navigating for the whole force. To their front the desert lay bare and ominous. To von Dodenburg's rear, the tanks were strung out over two kilometres, with a space of two hundred metres between each vehicle. Each tank and halftrack was followed by a plume of sand, highlighted by the slanting rays of the morning sun, as it pitched and rolled over the uneven surface. Von Dodenburg told himself they would make an ideal target for Tommy fighters – they could probably be seen for kilometres – but according to Rommel's staff, the British were not using fighters in this section of the front. He hoped the rear echelon stallions were right and concentrated on the task in hand.

The hours passed leadenly. At midday von Dodenburg allowed the men, bruised and exhausted by the violent progress of the vehicles, a ten minutes' break. After greedily drinking a quarter of his daily ration of two litres of water, which was to be used for all purposes, he made a quick inspection of his force. The tracks were holding up well, but the men were already beat. The heat, the dust and the motion of the vehicles were beginning to tell. The troopers were sprawled out full length in whatever shade they could find behind their vehicles, eyes closed, dead to the world, not even aware that their CO was looking down at them.

Schulze recognized von Dodenburg's concern. Recovered a little from the night before, he said: 'Don't worry about the wet-tails, sir! They'll make out.' He grinned suddenly. 'We'll break out that champagne we borrowed tonight. That'll perk 'em up.'

Von Dodenburg returned his grin. 'I don't know whether you'll make soldiers of them, Schulze, but you're going the right way to make them into drunkards.'

Schulze clapped his big hands around his mouth and bellowed. 'All right, you bunch of warm brothers masquerading as soldiers, up on those twinkle-toes! Make dust! Scratch a corner! Press on the tube. *LET'S GO!*' Their weary journey into the blank desert continued.

* * *

They were working their way through a very bad patch: an area of small boulders, filled in with solid tufts of scrub. As the 'Prof' had explained in his usual pedantic manner when they had entered it: 'One's usual conception of the desert is of an endless stretch of smooth sand rather like the dunes on the Baltic where one spent one's school vacations. But it is not like that at all. There are great variations in the topography – like this.'

Now the long column worked its way across the boulder-strewn ground, where every dip and hole was flattened to the eye by the almost perpendicular rays of the burning sun so that they cast no shadow to warn the drivers. The result was that the drivers could not avoid the crashing bumps, and the weary, sweat-lathered crews could not brace themselves in time. Thus the tanks and halftracks rattled and swayed their way forward with painful slowness, making less than ten kilometres an hour, with von Dodenburg, his head rent by a violent headache, staring to their front grimly through red-rimmed eyes.

It was about four when Reichert announced through cracked lips, 'Another kilometre and we should be out of it. According to the charts – and they're not very reliable naturally – the terrain returns to what the layman might call normal thereafter.'

'Good,' von Dodenburg said. He pressed his throat mike. 'Matz, hit the tube. I want to get ahead of the rest of the column and see what the ground ahead is like. We might be able to make another couple of hours before dark, if it's suitable.' He could hear Matz's hollow groan from the depths of the tank, but the little corporal replied dutifully enough: 'Yes sir.'

Next instant they started to draw away from the rest of the column, to which Schulze was already signalling to maintain the present speed. For half a kilometre or so, Matz kept the tank at a steady twenty-five kilometres an hour, in spite of the terrible terrain. But then they hit a long ascent and he was forced to climb it in low gear.

It was fortunate for Wotan that he did so. For just before they breasted the rise, von Dodenburg had time to spot what lay waiting for them below and cry urgently, '*Halt!*' Matz hit the brakes in a flash and they jarred to a bone-shaking stop.

'*Christ on a crutch*,' Schulze gasped, all breath knocked out of him. '*The buck-teethed Tommies!*'

TWO

Von Dodenhurg lowered his glasses and announced grimly, 'It looks as if they're going to settle in there for the night, Schulze.'

The big NCO nodded his agreement. 'You're right, sir. Look at 'em down there with those baggy long drawers of theirs, boiling up more of that tea-shit that they always swig by the litre. They're settling in, as if they're gonna be there forever!'

Von Dodenhurg took one last long look at the British positions: a circle of armoured cars and light tanks, with men squatting round blue-flickering petrol fires, while the officers gathered round the radio truck for some sort of conference. He made his decision. 'We'll have to attack, Schulze. Come on, let's get back to the tank and get on with it.

Bodies bent low, the two men scurried back to the command tank, which was now dug in in the hull-down position in the centre of the others. The commanders, poised alertly on their turrets, looked at him anxiously and von Dodenburg placed his hand on top of his khaki cap, fingers outstretched in the infantry signal for them to rally on him (he had ordered complete radio silence one hour before). A moment later they had dropped from their turrets and came doubling over to where the CO stood.

'All right, we are going to attack. For two reasons. One, we can't waste any more time here. Two. Now that they've stopped their own motors, they're bound to hear us, even if we did attempt to sneak our way round them.' He paused and glanced around at the dust-covered faces. Their weariness seemed to have vanished almost instantly and their red-rimmed eyes gleamed with sudden excitement. Young and as inexperienced as they were, they were obviously eager for battle. Von Dodenburg noted the point gratefully. 'Now most of you are new to battle,' he continued, 'and I don't want you taking any foolish risks. So this is the way we're going to do it. I shall take my tank up to the top of the ridge and show myself. My guess is that the Tommies will assume there is only a lone tank facing them and although that tank outguns those 37mm popguns their vehicles are armed with, they'll have a crack at me with their light tanks. Once they start their motors, you start up. Meier, you'll command the left wing. Seitz, the right.'

The two 18-year second-lieutenants snapped to attention.

'Once I open up with my 75, you will come in from the flanks in a wide swoop and envelop them like this.' He drew in his arms as if he were hugging a girl in a passionate embrace. 'You Sergeant Doerr.'

'Sir,' the one-eyed veteran NCO in charge of the panzer grenadiers barked.

'As soon as the two flanks go in, I shall advance down the slope and you'll follow with your halftracks.'

'*Jawohl, Hauptsturm*,' Doerr snapped. 'My boys'll tickle up those Tommies' asses for you, sir.'

'I don't want their asses just tickled,' von Dodenburg answered with unusual severity. 'Understand this – all of you. I want all those unfortunate Tommies killed. Not one of them must escape. All right, be off with you – and the best of luck.'

'Best of luck to you, too, sir,' they replied breathlessly and doubled back to their tanks.

Wotan was going to battle again!

* * *

'All right, Matz. Start up – *now!*' The 300 HP engines burst into life with a tremendous roar. Matz thrust home the gear and the tank rattled to the brow of the hill. Down below the Tommies had spun round to discover the cause of the sudden row. If what was going to happen next had not been so tragic, von Dodenburg could have burst out laughing at the comic look of surprise on their gawping British faces.

It seemed to take them an age to react to the appearance of an enemy tank in their midst. Then suddenly a white-haired man dropped the canteen from which he was drinking, and started to pelt for the radio truck with surprising speed for such an elderly man. 'Stop him, Schulze,' von Dodenburg rapped.

Schulze crouched behind the 75mm, pressed the trigger of one of the machine-guns almost automatically. A burst of tracer zipped flatly across the desert. The elderly officer faltered, flung up his hands dramatically, and flopped to the ground. The burst of machine-gun fire finally roused the British. They scattered in sudden alarm. Drivers tumbled into their tanks. Gunners flung themselves behind their weapons. Officers and NCOs barked hasty orders. In an instant, all was confusion and movement.

'Ten o'clock – radio truck – HE!' von Dodenburg barked.

Schulze swung the 75 round. He had already loaded the high explosive shell. The circle of the sight flew along the line of tanks and trucks. It settled on the radio truck, whose driver was frantically attempting to start it. Schulze centred the calibrated lines on the rear of the truck in which the radio equipment was housed. He hesitated for a fraction of a second and then pulled the firing lever.

The big 75 erupted. A spurt of purple flame shot from its muzzle. The turret was filled with the stink of burnt explosive, and the steaming empty shell-case came clattering out of the breech into the waiting collector bag.

Just as the first of the British light tanks started to climb towards them, the radio truck disappeared in a vicious flame and began to burn furiously. No one got out.

The leading Tommy tank was handicapped because it had to shoot uphill and the rays of the setting sun were in the eyes of the gunner and driver. Von Dodenburg ignored the first 37mm shell which flung up a fountain of sand and stones a dozen metres away which showered down on them like heavy rain on the turret. He had to lure the Tommies to an attack on the lone intruder before he threw in his two wings. 'Hold fast!' he ordered above the racket and grabbed the shaking side of the turret as the Matilda fired again and the Mark IV swayed with the impact of the near-miss like a ship at sea.

'Oh, my goodness,' the 'Prof' quavered, 'these things can be dangerous'.

'Quite,' von Dodenburg agreed and ducked instinctively as a 37mm shell struck the turret a resounding hollow blow and went whizzing off, unable to penetrate the thick armour.

He nudged Schulze's broad, sweat-soaked back. 'All right, Schulze, let him have it now,' he commanded. 'They've bought it.'

Schulze swung the great sinister hooded gun round. From von Dodenburg's position on the turret it seemed at least ten metres long. He grunted and pulled the firing lever. The white blob of the AP shell hit the British tank squarely in the engine. For a moment nothing happened. The tank still continued its laborious crawl up the steep hill. *Whoosh!* The Matilda's petrol tank exploded. In an instant it was a blazing inferno. With a thick asthmatic crump, its ammunition racks exploded, piercing the black oily smoke with a stab of violent scarlet flame.

A man staggered out of the lower escape hatch. His face was pitch-black and both his clothes and hair were alight. He stumbled a few metres, his legs getting progressively heavier; then he fell and in a frenzy of agony rolled back and forth on the hard sand in a desperate attempt to put out the flames. His flailing, tormented arms and legs moved more slowly. With a convulsive heave, he lay still.

Von Dodenburg made his decision. The whole of the British tank force, followed by the armoured cars, was now advancing up the hill to where the stricken Matilda blazed away fiercely. 'Matz,' he cried through the throat mike, 'advance! ...Schulze!'

'Sir?'

'Fire at will!'

As Matz thrust home his gears and began to rumble towards the attacking force, von Dodenburg heard the roar of the concealed tanks and halftracks starting up their engines. The trap had been well and truly sprung!

★ ★ ★

It was a massacre. The Tommies realized too late that they had walked into a trap. The armoured cars tried to break away, relying on their superior speed to escape, but they could not evade the two young second-lieutenants' gunners. One by one, the 76s knocked them out. Soon a couple of square kilometres of desert were littered with the burning armoured cars.

Von Dodenburg, followed by the panzer grenadiers' halftracks, charged straight into the mass of British tanks. Schulze firing from right to left, smashed Matilda after Matilda to a flaming standstill, while Sergeant Doerr's young grenadiers mercilessly mowed down those of the crews who managed to escape.

Here and there individual Tommies tried to stop the German advance, standing in the path of the metal monsters and attempting to hold them off with rifles and revolvers. But within seconds they disappeared screaming under the churning tank tracks to fall behind – mutilated chunks of flesh in the bloody sand.

Eventually von Dodenburg had had enough of the slaughter. 'Stop firing!' he cried thickly, sickened by the bloodshed, but knowing that there was more – and worse – to come.

He turned and repressing the wave of nausea that threatened to overcome him at the sight of his blood-red tracks, through which protruded a severed naked arm, the fingers outstretched as if pleading with God for mercy. He signalled to Doerr to do what had to be done.

Wearily he closed his eyes and slumped against the hot metal of the turret. He tried to ignore the whimpering pleas for mercy, and cries of fear of the Tommies, which always ended in the sharp crack of Doerr's revolver; but he failed lamentably. Every time the revolver cracked, he twitched convulsively.

Next to him, the 'Prof' whispered over and over again, '*Oh my blessed Saviour…oh my blessed Saviour!*'

One hour later they moved on, leaving behind them the silent heaps of dead and the still burning tanks, outlined a sombre black against the blood-red ball of the setting sun.

Major von Dodenburg, his face pale and buried deep in the collar of his greatcoat in the sudden night chill, did not look back. *He couldn't!*

THREE

On the afternoon of the second day, Wotan entered the Sand Sea. At first the going was good, apart from a couple of bad patches of soft sand. But towards evening they ran into a series of dunes which swept to the darkening horizon. Most were razor-backed and it demanded a great deal of skill on the part of the driver to traverse them.

Matz soon showed that he had an excellent eye for terrain and just what an experienced driver he was. He had the special technique at his finger-tips. He would position the tank at the base of the dune and charge at the mountain of sand at full speed. Just before the tank was about to lurch alarmingly over the top of the dune, perhaps to face a sheer drop of ten or twenty metres on the other side, he would jam on the brakes, swing the steering round violently and rattle down the other side at a frightening, hair-raising angle.

Some of the other drivers, especially those in the halftracks which did not have equivalent traction, were not so successful in their attempts to surmount the dunes. Regularly a cursing driver would get bogged down helplessly in the sand. Then the rest of the crew would have to get out and begin the back-breaking task of freeing the tracks and digging holes beneath them so that the metal sand channels could be placed underneath to allow the trapped vehicle more traction.

That afternoon they hardly made twenty-five kilometres, and by nightfall von Dodenburg had had enough. He called a halt and told the crews to prepare their evening meal. The men formed the defensive laager for the night and dropped onto the sand, exhausted, grateful for the start of the night breeze after the murderous heat of that day.

Von Dodenburg supervised the activities of his own crew and while the 'Prof' and Schulze set about preparing the evening meal, he decided to 'take the spade for a walk'.

With the spade over his shoulder and a wad of newspaper in the other, he slogged up the nearest dune and down the other side. There out of sight of the camp, he emptied his bowels and was just about to begin using the spade when he caught the glint of glass a long way away.

For a moment he thought his eyes were playing him tricks after the strain and glare of the long day. But then he saw it again. He dropped his spade and fumbled for his own binoculars. But he was an instant too late. At that moment the sun slipped beneath the horizon and the desert was plunged into darkness. The gleam had vanished.

Thoughtfully, von Dodenburg walked back to the busy little camp. Someone had been watching him out there. The question was – *who?*

★ ★ ★

In spite of his exhaustion, von Dodenburg awoke at two and could not get to sleep again. He was due to relieve 'Prof' at three for his hour of guard-duty anyway, so he lay there, hands propped underneath his head, staring at the cold silver infinity of the stars and listening to the singing of the sand. For a while he lay there – planning the next day and glancing at the dial of his wrist-watch.

Then, by instinct, he unzipped his sleeping bag. Shuddering a little in the night cold, he pulled on his desert boots, flung his black leather jacket around his shoulders and clambered on to the turret in which the 'Prof' was keeping watch.

'You're early, Major,' the 'Prof' whispered, obviously not wishing to disturb the men snoring heartily all round.

'Couldn't sleep any more, Prof,' von Dodenburg answered.

For a few minutes the two officers stood there in silence, staring up at the stars which seemed low enough to touch. Then von

Dodenburg broke the silence. 'Prof, I'd like to ask you a question. Does anyone live out here in this miserable wilderness?' Swiftly von Dodenburg explained what he thought he had seen the night before, almost doubting his testimony as he did so.

Reichert seemed to take a long time before he answered. 'It is a long story, Major,' he said finally. 'You know that there is a theory that the Sahara is constantly expanding outwards. Once, it is thought, this was probably the bread basket of the Ancient World, an exceedingly fertile place, though it is hard to believe now, is it not?

'Be that as it may, a combination of changing trade winds and the fact that the Romans chopped down most of the forests on the littoral to obtain timber for their galleys changed the whole weather picture of the area. The rains washed the humus from the fertile fields, leaving the bare rock which eventually turned into sand. With no vegetation, there was no rain. So we have an arid, barren area which cannot support much in the way of population. The people began to leave. But not all. Some remained behind and because of the climatic conditions they changed from peaceful farmers into robbers, men who preyed off the coastal settlements and who had their own laws and customs, completely different from those of their brothers who had moved north. Two thousand years later, Major von Dodenburg, they are still out here, having in the meantime become more vicious and stranger in their ways.'

'But how do they live?' von Dodenburg asked, intrigued by the fact that men actually lived in this burning sand waste.

'Just as their forefathers lived. Raping and plundering. I'm afraid it's a little beyond my own particular province, Major,' the 'Prof' continued, 'but I have heard that in this section of what you choose to call a miserable wilderness, there lives the Blue Veil People.'

'Blue Veil People?' von Dodenburg echoed 'A strange name!'

'And a strange people, too, Major. Like the Toureg, the men veil themselves. But for different reasons. The Blue Veil are, I regret to say, given to the English perversion.'

'You mean homosexuality?'

'I do.'

'But how do they continue as a tribe,' von Dodenburg objected, 'If they're warm brothers? Where do the kids come from?'

'At regular intervals prescribed by their tribal laws, they seize women and procreate. In the mid-thirties the Italians had a great deal of trouble with them when they began to carry off the wives of the Italian settlers. But in essence they find the Greek vice a more noble form of sexual activity.... But do not be misled by the fact that they are homosexual,' the 'Prof' pronounced the word as if it were in quotation marks – 'they are a bold, brave and completely ruthless tribe.'

'So you think I might well have seen a Blue Veil out there?'

'You might indeed.'

'And on whose side are they?' von Dodenburg queried, 'The Italians' or the Tommies'?'

Reichert's leathery face cracked in a weary smile. He made a gesture signifying money. 'On the side of those who pay most, my dear Major. And now I think it is time for me to retire for what is left of the night.' With that he was gone, leaving Major von Dodenburg staring into the desert, as if he could already visualize the strange, veiled tribesmen crawling towards the sleeping encampment.

FOUR

Next morning von Dodenburg's sense of foreboding had disappeared. The sky was perfect and the air was cool. Followed by Schulze, he strode purposefully from vehicle to vehicle checking them and their crews, ensuring that the drivers turned over the engines with the starting handle to avoid any chance of damage to the bottom cylinder by a hydrostatic lock.

By six, the column was on its way again, ploughing ever further into the depths of the uncharted sand-sea.

Now the character of the desert started to change. The razor-edged dunes gave way to rough terrain, broken here and there by flat-topped hills. The column picked up speed, much to von Dodenburg's pleasure. All the same he was worried by the terrain; ideal country for an ambush. Leaving the navigation completely to the 'Prof' and guiding of the column to Schulze, he scanned the desert ahead constantly with his binoculars for any sign of life. It remained empty. At midday, after covering nearly forty kilometres, von Dodenburg ordered a thirty minutes halt. While Schulze and Matz cooked looted Australian sausages over the petrol-and-sand fire on the blade of a shovel, von Dodenburg and the 'Prof' conferred over the map. But von Dodenburg could see the other man's mind was elsewhere and finally he asked: 'Come on, Prof, what is it? You've got a face like forty days' rain.'

The 'Prof' pointed to the sky. 'Look at that.'

The sky was the colour of wood smoke. From it the sun shone

down like a coin seen dimly at the bottom of a dirty country pool. 'Well?' he demanded.

'Do you not notice, Major, that the wind has stopped blowing? Well, all the signs are there, my dear Major,' the 'Prof' said severely, pursing his cracked lips.

'All the signs of what?' von Dodenburg barked, biting into a red-hot sausage.

'Sand storm!'

* * *

The sand storm hit them one hour later. A gust of wind hit the tank with such force that it shuddered violently. In an instant it was as black as night. 'I told you so!' the 'Prof' screamed above the sudden vicious howl.

'Oh shut up!' von Dodenburg yelled. He grabbed the mike. 'Commander to all vehicles,' he roared above the ever increasing howl, trying to ignore the sand particles striking his face like angry hailstones, 'Proceed to the high ground at two o'clock and stop motors! I repeat – high ground at two o'clock and stop motors. Over and out!' He dropped the mike and ducked behind the cover of the turret as the sandstorm struck the column at 150 kilometres an hour. Next to him Schulze howled with pain as the flying sand particles cut into his broad face like a myriad, red-hot stilettos.

The rest of the column vanished in the whirling storm of sand. Breathing became difficult. Von Dodenburg felt as if he were being garrotted. The hellish fog of sand snatched the air from his lungs. Next to him Schulze and the 'Prof' were choking for breath like asthmatics.

Pulling down his sand-goggles, von Dodenburg glanced over the turret. If the rest of his force was there somewhere, he could not see them. They had vanished into the flying wall of sand. For all he knew they were all alone in this crazy anarchic world. Full of apprehension he ducked his head behind cover again.

Somehow Matz managed to drive on, while the wind shrieked furiously across the desert, as if some God on high had ordained that these puny mortals, who had had the temerity to venture into this burning world, should be wiped from the face of the earth.

Over the intercom von Dodenburg heard Matz curse. The Mark IV lurched to a stop. Had Matz managed to reach the ridge at two o'clock? Or had something broken down? At that moment, von Dodenburg neither knew nor cared. Nothing mattered, save the task of surviving the elemental fury of the storm.

Then as suddenly as it had started, the storm declined. The terrifying howl gave way to a lower keening, which soon disappeared altogether, leaving behind an echoing silence.

Like blind men the soldiers in the turret stretched out their hands to feel their bodies. Von Dodenburg rubbed his sand-goggles clean. Next to him Schulze and the 'Prof' were clearing away the thick layer of sand which covered their bodies. He stood up, sand pouring from his body and stared over the turret.

The desert was transformed. The ridge he had directed his vehicles to had inexplicably vanished. So had the rest of the column. They were alone.

'Christ Almighty!' he cursed and pressed his throat mike urgently. 'Matz, get the thing started up again. We've got to find the rest of the column – at once,' he ordered.

'Sorry, sir,' Matz's voice came over the intercom. 'I think we've shot a track. I'm getting no traction.'

'*Scheisse!* All right, Matz, I'll have a look.'

Swiftly von Dodenburg dropped over the side into the sand which had buried the lower track. He grubbed away the sand the whole length of the track, trying to find the source of trouble. Then he found it. Something had caught a connecting pin and had twisted it out of all recognition. One of the pin's jagged ends had been carried over the sprocket wheel until it had become embedded in the sand-shield on that side of the tank? Now there was a mass of tangled metal stuck there.

Matz joined von Dodenburg. 'What a shitty mess!'

'What a shitty mess, indeed!' von Dodenburg agreed.

For a few minutes the two of them stood there surveying the

wreckage in silence until Matz said: 'It can be fixed, sir. But it'll take a bit of time. And I'll need that big Hamburg ox up there to give me a hand.'

'All right,' von Dodenburg made a quick decision. 'Prof you give these two rogues here a bit of cover. I'm going to see if I can find the others. They can't have got far,' he added hopefully. He pulled down a water bottle and slung it over his shoulder next to his machine pistol. 'If I don't find them in the next fifteen minutes, I'll come back and give you a hand. We'll try to raise the rest of the Company by radio, though God knows how I'll be able to give them a fix on us when I don't know where the hell we are.' With that he started on his search.

★ ★ ★

He could barely hear the clang of Schulze's sledge hammer on the jammed metal and the tank itself was hidden behind a ridge. He glanced at his watch. He had already been walking ten minutes. But there was still no sign of the rest of the column. Von Dodenburg frowned with irritation. Had they gone blundering on, blinded by the storm, and thinking that the command tank was still in the lead?

'Damn the two of them,' he cursed the 18-year-old second-lieutenants. 'They should have tumbled to the fact that we're missing by –' The angry words died on his lips.

On the far horizon, a line of dark figures had suddenly appeared. He breathed a sigh of relief and pulling his binoculars out of their case, focused them hurriedly.

He saw immediately that they were not his men. The strangers, strung out in a long line, were dressed in the flowing robes of the desert Arab and they were riding on camels. He adjusted the glasses more finely and tried to pick out the details of the first rider. Suddenly he gasped and lowered the glasses hurriedly. An instant later he was running heavily through the soft sand the way he had come. *The leading rider's face was covered by a blue veil!*

FIVE

Von Dodenburg tensed over the radio. 'Here Sunray…here Sunray,' he called desperately…. 'Do you read me, over?' He flicked the mike switch and waited anxiously, while the other three stared up at him in taut anticipation.

There was no answering crackle.

Angrily he thrust the mike back on its hook. 'The damned fools must be on radio silence – or something equally idiotic,' he snapped.

'What now?' the 'Prof asked.

Von Dodenburg straightened up and stared out of the turret. The horizon was still empty. 'All right,' he decided, 'we'll continue working.' He unslung his machine pistol and slapped it in the 'Prof's' unwilling hands. 'I'm going to help Schulze and Matz. You stand guard.'

'But I've never fired one of these,' Reichart protested. 'I don't know how it works.'

'Well, now is obviously a good time to find out,' von Dodenburg cried, seizing the pin and holding it against the jammed part, while Schulze grunted and brought down the sledgehammer.

One blow sufficed. The track-pin parted and landed with a tinkle of metal on the pebbles, while the sound of the sledge echoed and re-echoed across the desert. Von Dodenburg dropped the other pin. Close at hand he heard the crackle of camel-thorn, or so he thought. He straightened up; the horizon was still empty. All the same, every nerve of his body tensed for the shock of discovery and rattle of rifle-fire which would follow. Surely the Arabs must have heard! He tried to dismiss the Blue Veils from his mind and snapped: 'All right, Schulze, grab one of the crowbars! Matz, Schulze and I will lift up the sandshield, you grab the track. When I say "heave" – *heave!*'

Matz nodded. He took hold of the severed piece of track and prepared to pull, while von Dodenburg and Schulze thrust the crowbars underneath the sand-shield. The Major spat on his palms and commanded: 'One, two, three – *heave!*'

There was a rending, metallic sound which von Dodenburg thought must have been heard for kilometres, but still Matz was unable to pull the trapped section free.

'Christ on a crutch!' Schulze roared in sudden anger at Matz. 'What are you – a shitty pygmy or something? Too much wanking, Matzi, that's your trouble. Sapping your strength you are!'

Von Dodenburg glanced at the horizon. It was still empty, thank God! 'Come on,' he gasped, 'let's save our breath and get on with it!'

Twice more they tried to free the section of trapped track and twice they failed. By now von Dodenburg's nerves were jangling. His imagination was prey to every terror. Shapes which he had marked out of the corner of his eyes as bushes or patches of camel-thorn suddenly moved or disappeared. New shapes appeared momentarily where there had been none before.

'Come on,' he croaked, wiping away the beads of sweat which threatened to blind him, 'let's have another go at the sodding thing!'

Angrily the three of them took up their positions once more. 'Now *HEAVE!*' von Dodenburg cried.

There was the searing sound of metal freeing itself and then Matz was lying on his back in the sand, with a length of track draped across his skinny body. Slowly the rest of the track slithered over the runners and flopped to the ground like a suddenly severed limb.

Schulze dropped his crowbar and glared at Matz, pinned down by the weight of the track. 'Well, don't just lie there, you cripple, like a pissy-assed spare prick in a convent. Getup!'

'I can't,' Matz said through gritted teeth. 'I've got this shitty thing on my chest, you stupid bastard!'

'Quick,' von Dodenburg ordered. 'There's no time to be lost!' Together the two men pulled the length of damaged track off Matz's chest and then ran to the spares' bin. Schulze grunted, and exerting all his tremendous strength, hauled out a replacement section of track. He dropped it to the ground. Swiftly the men went to work to fit the new section.

While von Dodenburg sweated and strained to loosen the idler wheel adjustment, Matz and Schulze linked the new part to the old track and started to thread it across the runners once more. The noise the three of them made was tremendous. But von Dodenburg knew it could not be helped. The Blue Veils would discover them soon and even behind the 80mm armour they would not be safe from them. It was an old adage in Assault Regiment Wotan that an immobilized tank was nothing better than a coffin, once it was surrounded by determined infantry. A carefully placed hand grenade would ensure that the biggest tank was soon dead. Thus he laboured with the others, sweating and cursing, expecting Reichert's shout of warning at any moment.

It came in a frightened quaver. 'Major...Major von Dodenburg, *look!*' The 'Prof' pointed a skinny finger, which trembled visibly, to the horizon.

On the horizon, silhouetted against the setting sun like some classical frieze, twenty or more of the riders were strung out in a long line gazing down at them in silence.

'What shall I do?' the 'Prof' asked fearfully. 'They're the Blue Veils all right.'

'Don't worry, Prof. Those rifles have – at the most – a range of a hundred metres. And they're more than two hundred away. If they get closer, give them a quick burst.' While the three of them continued in their desperate attempts to link the two sections of track, a group of the Blue Veils dismounted from the camels. Under the command of an Arab they began to unpack a shining cylindrical object from the back of one of the kneeling pack-camels.

Just as the three SS men managed to pull the two sections of track together and Schulze started to hammer home the link-pin, von Dodenburg glanced at the Blue Veils. His heart sank. The Arabs were setting up a mortar on the heights, and if they did not get under way quickly, they would be sitting ducks in the hollow at that range. He had underestimated the Blue Veils.

'*Mortar!*' he gasped.

'I'll get the pincers,' Matz cried. 'You fit the cotter-pin, Schulze.'

'No time,' the sweating giant cried through gritted teeth. He inserted the pin which held the track-link in place and taking a deep breath, he turned it with his powerful fingers, feeling metal dig deep into his flesh as he did so. 'That'll do,' he yelled and kicked the track with his big boot. It held. 'Come on, get the lead out of your ass, Matzi! Into that driving compartment!' Matz saw the danger at once. He scrambled for the driving seat, while von Dodenburg and Schulze clambered onto the turret.

The light mortar opened up with a cough and a frightening howl. Crouched in the turret, the SS men could see the black blob of the mortar bomb wobbling downwards through the darkening sky. It exploded with a thick crump. Sand shot skywards, some twenty metres away and showered the tank with pebbles and small boulders. They ducked instinctively.

On the ridge, the Blue Veils under the direction of the little Arab made an adjustment and re-loaded. Down below in the green-glowing driving compartment, Matz completed all his frantic starting checks. Just as the second mortar bomb began to howl towards them, he pressed the starter-button. *Nothing happened!*

SIX

Schulze swept the ridge with the machine-gun, but the Blue Veils had anticipated that. They had dragged their camels hurriedly behind the cover of the height and after a moment's pause had begun firing once more from beyond it; and from the way the first bomb came winging down only a dozen metres away, von Dodenburg realized with a sinking feeling that the man who was directing the firing knew his mortars.

Below Matz wrestled with the engines. Frantically he pressed the starter time and time again. But it would not start. Desperately von Dodenburg clenched his fists in anxiety and willed the shitty monster to fire. Soon he knew the little Arab would get lucky and land a bomb right on the turret, or on top of the engines. Even if they survived the explosion, which was unlikely, then they would be easy meat for Blue Veil infiltrators. Matz had to start the engines!

Cursing furiously, Matz fought to start up. And then he had it. There was a long, low groan like some eerie unearthly dirge. Von Dodenburg glanced to the rear, just as another mortar bomb landed so close that the blast ripped the shovel clipped to the turret away. A stream of black smoke was pouring from the twin exhausts. Matz was doing it. He pressed his throat mike urgently. 'It's working, Matz,' he cried. '*Come on…come on!*'

The noise grew in intensity. The Mark IV shivered violently. Its every plate rattled, as if it might fall apart at any moment. An ashen-faced 'Prof' hung on grimly, his lips moving rapidly in prayer. A sharp series of backfires. A burst of bright white smoke. Next moment the twin engines roared into full life. Frantically Matz gunned the engines, and slammed home the gear.

Just as the bomb intended to land right on the trapped tank's turret came hurtling down out of the dark sky with a stomach-churning howl, the big tank lurched forward. With his engines still not reliable enough for him to brake and turn, Matz made his own decision and rolled straight ahead, right into the Blue Veils' positions.

Too late to brake, too late to slow down, the 25-ton monster shot over the ridge. In panic the Arabs around the mortar scattered. A boy fell screaming under the tracks and Matz caught a quick glimpse of rouged cheeks and painted eyebrows, before he was dragged under, churned to a bloody pulp of flesh and bone by the great tracks. However, he had no time for the Blue Veils. His whole energy was concentrated on keeping the tank from overturning on the almost sheer descent which had suddenly loomed up before his horrified gaze.

The left-hand track hit a hidden boulder with a bone-shuddering impact. Instinctively Matz braked the track. In a blinding flurry of sand, the tank swerved to the left. Somehow Matz managed to keep control with hands that were dripping with sweat, as it began to slither sidewards down the slope. One false move now and they would be over. Behind them the Arabs lying in the sand were taking wild angry shots.

Gingerly Matz started to brake the right track. The Mark IV wobbled violently. Sand showered up from the tracks. They were only a matter of metres from the bottom of the descent now. Matz exerted more pressure on the right track. It screamed as it churned up sand. Matz tensed for the bone-breaking crash that must come. A huge wake of flying sand was following their progress down the slope in a hellish howl of protesting metal. Then the track caught. Revolving frantically, showering up stones and rocks, the other track caught hold. They started to swing around. Matz pressed his foot down hard on the gas pedal, and chanced more pressure on the right track. The Mark IV did not let him down. Now it swung right round and in a flash they were hurtling down the steep incline, with Matz holding on the controls, his stomach seemingly floating somewhere high above his sweat-drenched head.

Just before the tank ran full-tilt into the depression, Matz braked, let go, and braked again. The trick worked. They hit the bottom at less than ten kilometres an hour. At any other speed, it would have shattered there. Just before the tank came to rest, Matz tapped the accelerator. The twin engines responded at once.

They throbbed sweetly and swiftly built up power. The tracks bit into the soft sand of the ascent on the other side. *They held!* Matz breathed a sigh of relief. Slowly but surely, the battered Panzerkampfwagen IV started to climb while behind them the sound of the Blue Veils' firing grew fainter and fainter. They had escaped!

Thirty minutes later they bumped into the stalled Italian truck, its back filled with the Italian soldiers Schulze had kidnapped from the quay. They were drunk and unhappy, eating sticky chocolate sandwiches and drinking the Chianti they had stolen from the German Supply Depot. They were lost too and frightened, very frightened.

For a moment von Dodenburg was bewildered. While Matz and Schulze grabbed what was left of the Chianti, he leaned weakly against the side of the truck, drained of energy. However, the crackle of the radio in the truck's cabin soon shook him out of his reverie.

By some stroke of good fortune, the Italians' radio was on the column's net!

Thrusting the anxious Italians out of the way, von Dodenburg grabbed the mike and bellowed into it. 'Hello, here Sunray…here Sunray. Are you reading me? …'

One hour later they had rejoined the column.

SEVEN

Angrily Slaughter scooped out the two yolks of the precious fried eggs with his fingers, Arab-fashion, and swallowed them. By the light of the flickering camel-dung fire, Yassa looked at him silently and thoughtfully, smoking his cigarette in the Mohammedan manner so that his lips did not come in contact with the tobacco, as the Prophet had prescribed. He was an incredibly wrinkled old man beneath his blue veil, his eyebrows plucked in what he thought was a seductive curve and great smears of *kohl* below the tired yellow eyes. Yet if the Blue Veil Chiefs face and manner were pathetic attempts at female coquettism, there was nothing weak or unmasculine about his determination. Stretching one painted hand to the warmth of the fire, he said: 'We shall ride all day and all night. We might not catch them the night of the morrow, nor the night of the day after that.'

'When?' Slaughter demanded angrily, stubbing out his cigarette in the white of one of the fried eggs, as if he were grinding out the socket.

'Do not worry, my friend,' the Chief answered easily. 'We shall earn your Horsemen. Perhaps in three nights.'

'*When?*' Slaughter persisted. He knew his Blue Veils, his 'boys' as he always called them to his superiors in Cairo. One had to pin them down; they were as skittish and as capricious as women.

'Three nights, I have said,' the Chief replied. 'Like all infidels, they will rest at night. We will not. We will catch them, Englishman, and then –' The Chief grinned at him over his veil, though there was no real warmth in his faded old eyes. 'Then,' he echoed, 'we shall ensure that they never leave the desert.'

Slaughter shuddered in spite of the fact that the Blue Veils had been his lovers and employees ever since he had begun to use them for espionage purposes against the Italians in Libya in 1935. They would slit the Germans' throats and unspeakable atrocities would follow that. Slaughter, his voice suddenly dry and husky, asked: 'Where?'

'The Great Ascent,' the Chief said simply and with a gesture of finality tossed his cigarette into the fire. It flared up for a moment, illuminating the old man's perverted face, and eyes which flashed with cruel anticipation of the slaughter to come.

SECTION THREE:

THE OASIS

'Madam is the bravest of the brave. Not even Nasser and Sadat surpass her in courage and hatred of the English.'

Major Mustafa, Egyptian Army, to
von Dodenburg, Ain Dalla Oasis

ONE

It was furnace-hot. In that heat the sand shimmered a crazy wavering blue. Wearily the column steered its way onwards.

'It's the khamsin,' the 'Prof' explained through cracked lips. 'Blows in from Central Africa across hundreds of kilometres, being heated more and more all the way.'

Von Dodenburg had never experienced a wind like this before, not even in the Caucasus. It was not like the heat that came from the sun, from which there was some relief in the shade. The khamsin was a searing, blistering heat that made one blink with shock, as if an oven door had been flung open to release a fearsome blast of burning air.

'Jesus, Mary, Joseph!' Schulze groaned, 'you'd think it was bad enough with the Tommies and those Niggers out there somewhere trying to croak us – without this shitting wind roasting the nuts off us!'

The almost unbearable heat was also making the young drivers of the sections of the column commanded by the two 18-year-old second-lieutenants more and more careless. Time and time again they drove into patches of soft sand because they were not alert enough and the whole column had to stop while the trapped vehicles were dugout.

In the end, when yet another of Seitz's Mark IVs became bogged down in soft sand, von Dodenburg's temper got the better of him. He stopped the column, ordered Matz to drive back to where the weary young tank crew were staring numbly at the vehicle, which was up to its bogies in sand, and bellowed 'Seitz and Meier to me – at the double!' Both officers dropped from their vehicles and shambled wearily across to where von Dodenburg stood grimly on the turret, hands clamped to his hips. '*At the double!*' he bellowed again. 'Get the lead out of your damn tails, will you!'

Sergeant Doerr, whose halftracks had not bogged down once because his drivers were exceedingly scared of him, guffawed. But the rest of the Wotan men were too weary to laugh even at the sight of two red-faced, sweat-lathered officers doubling through the sand as if they were green recruits back at *Sennalager*. Gasping painfully, their shirts black with sweat, the two of them came to a halt in front of von Dodenburg and stood to attention.

Von Dodenburg's red-rimmed eyes flashed angrily. 'You call yourselves officers,' he barked bitterly. 'Officer means someone who commands, leads, makes decisions, advises. You two pathetic creatures have done none of those things. You have idled in your turrets and allowed your men to make the decisions – the wrong ones. That's why tank after tank of yours has bogged down. Well, I have had enough of it. You must be taught to be officers the hard way!'

He turned to the crestfallen corporal in charge of the tank which had bogged down. 'All right, get all of your crew except the driver out of there, corporal!' The crewmen dropped to the sand and stood staring up at their crimson-faced CO. 'Corporal, clip off the turret shovels and give them to the officers!'

Silently the Corporal did as he was commanded and stood to one side, leaving the young officers staring down at the implements in embarrassed bewilderment.

'Now, you two. You will clear the sand away from this one by yourselves till the driver can start,' von Dodenburg. announced grimly, 'and you will clear away the sand from every other one of your vehicles that bogs down after this, *personally and unaided!* Perhaps that will teach you both to ensure that your drivers and commanders don't sleep at their posts. Now get on with it!'

Embarrassed, hurt, on the brink of tears, the two young officers began the back-breaking task of clearing the tracks, watched by equally embarrassed and sympathetic Wotan troopers.

Thereafter there was no further bogging down of vehicles in the rest of the column, but the mood among the men, von Dodenburg knew, was rebellious. He longed to reach the Ascent and leave the hell of the Great Sand Sea.

★ ★ ★

That morning passsed with leaden feet. At midday, von Dodenburg allowed the column to stop to prepare a meal. Here and there a soldier dropped to the sand gratefully and tried to urinate. But the exercise was very painful. Their kidneys had suffered too much from the batterings and joltings of the last four days and the men had to clutch the sides of the vehicles to fight back the burning pain as they emptied their bladders. For the most part, the men crouched where they were, all spirit knocked out of them by the hellish terrain.

Von Dodenburg dropped stiff-kneed to the sand and inspected his men. Their sweat-stained shirts were already bleached a faded yellow and their desert boots had turned near-white in the rays of the sun. Their faces were hollow and bronzed. Already they looked like veterans, as if they had been in the desert for years like the men of the *Afrikakorps*. But von Dodenburg knew that their appearance was deceptive. The men were not desert veterans; they were simply exhausted.

Behind him, the ever-present Schulze, who himself must have lost five kilos so that even his massive frame seemed shrunken, put the CO's thoughts into words. 'The wet-tails are knackered, sir. What they need is plenty of drink and to be out of this hellhole to wherever we're supposed to be going.' He looked curiously at the Major.

Von Dodenburg did not rise to the bait. Instead he grunted: 'Break out an extra half a litre this midday.' And with that he stalked off, leaving Schulze staring after him in angry bewilderment. Finally, the big NCO spun round and cupping his hands round his mouth shouted:

'All right, you bunch of lovely lads, Sergeant Major Schulze has got a treat for you! By special permission you can all have an extra half litre of camel-piss, known to you as water this afternoon!'

Later, concealed by a convenient dune and sharing his last bottle of champagne (Cooled expensively in a five litre can of gasoline) with Matz, he grunted moodily; 'I'd just like to know where we're going, Matzi? I really would!'

Matz pumped another squirt of the precious gas over the bottle propped in the sand to keep it cool and answered lazily, 'Wherever it is, Schulze, it can't be worse than this. Nothing can.'

'Ay,' Schulze said dourly, 'that's what you say. But I don't know so much.' He stared at the silent, shifting dunes all around and shivered, in spite of the tremendous heat. 'This shitting sandpit puts years on me Matzi…. Give me shitting old Timmerndorf[1] any day.'

★ ★ ★

That evening in their laager, revived a little by the cooler breeze of the night, the 'Prof' chided von Dodenburg in his stiff, professorial way, saying he felt that the young Major was too hard on his men.

Von Dodenburg stared at the elderly academic across the blue flickering flames of the gas fire and said harshly: 'You might be one of Germany's leading Egyptologists, Prof, but I'm afraid you know little of soldiering, especially the kind of soldiering we of the Armed SS are used to. We cannot sustain ourselves with hope, for there is no hope for the SS. We cannot sustain ourselves with thought — belief in a cause,' he uttered the words with a sneer — 'faith that there is ultimately something of worth in what we are doing. *There isn't!*

'Our sole purpose is to kill and *to avoid being killed ourselves*. The function of German industry is to put the weapons into our hands so that we can blow a hole in some unfortunate Russian or Tommy head. We exist as rock-bottom, guilty animals, who must be taught to survive, kill the other animal before he kills you.' His voice softened as he saw the horrified look on the other man's face and he concluded

---

1. A popular beach near Hamburg.

almost gently. 'The men must be hard as a favour to themselves, for the weak ones don't survive…' He emptied his coffee. 'Now let me change the subject.' He leaned forward so that none of the men could hear him. 'When will we reach the Ascent?' he asked.

'Is that where we are heading?'

Von Dodenburg nodded.

Professor Reichert's faded elderly eyes flickered, as if he were going to say something hastily, but evidently he thought better of it, for when he spoke he said simply:

'If my calculations are correct – early tomorrow evening.'

For a few moments von Dodenburg absorbed the information, listening to the soft sounds of the camp settling down for the night: the hiss of urine on the still sand; the clatter of canteens being put away; the lazy banter of men lying sleepily in their bags, talking of the things all soldiers talk about – war and women. Then he said: 'Prof, what can you tell me of the place?'

'The Ascent? There is not much I can tell you, Major. I've never been there myself. In my days in Egypt all this was named the Devil's Country and one kept out of it. Besides the handful of British who did penetrate it were not too happy about having Germans poking around it, especially after the Pact of Steel[2]. However this I do know. One of their officers – a certain Major Clayton seems to have discovered it, apart from the Arabs naturally who have probably always known about it, in the late twenties. According to the few descriptions I have heard of it, it is a great curving ramp of sand running up to a rock wall.'

Von Dodenburg nodded. It was roughly the same description that Rommel had given him. 'Can you tell me any more?' he asked. 'What are the conditions that we may be expected to face tomorrow night, for example?'

'Not very much, Major, I'm afraid. Narrow gullies, framed by high rocks which I would expect would be too steep and too high for your tanks to climb.'

---

2. Alliance between Mussolini and Hitler.

'You mean we shall leave the Great Sand Sea through some sort of gully feature, which is already known to the Tommies?'

'Yes indeed. After all we of *Afrikakorps* Intelligence have known that the British have been using the Ascent since 1940. Indeed *they* call it the "Easy Ascent".'

'So if they knew we were coming, that is one of the places they would be waiting for us?' von Dodenburg demanded with sudden urgency.

'Yes, that is if they had enough of their special desert troops to cover the spot, which according to Major Samt of *Afrikakorps* Intelligence they don't. They are all up at the front...' He stopped suddenly. The other man no longer seemed to be listening. For what seemed an age, von Dodenburg crouched there in front of the fire, lost in thought. Then he made up his mind. He rose to his feet. 'Sergeant-Major Schulze!' he called. 'Get me Sergeant Doerr of the panzer grenadiers at the double.'

'At the double, sir,' Schulze's huge voice came floating back through the glowing darkness.

Von Dodenburg looked at the 'Prof'. 'Now Doktor Reichert, I've got a little task for you this night before you sleep.'

'Major?'

'I would like you to prepare a route to the Ascent for a one-eyed sergeant, who isn't too bright,' von Dodenburg said with a smile on his face. 'And at the double, Prof, *if you please...*'

TWO

Von Dodenburg stared back along the column in the dawn light. There was a distance of fifty metres between each tank, as he prescribed the night before after they had reached the approach to the Ascent. He nodded to himself in satisfaction. His lesson had paid dividends. The two second-lieutenants had their crews well in hand now.

He turned and faced his front. The track which ran towards the Ascent was dangerously narrow – just broad enough for one vehicle – and as the 'Prof' had predicted, they were hemmed in on both sides. To their right, the naked rock wall rose steeply above them, while to their left the abyss fell away to an unknown depth, veiled still in the pre-dawn mist. The approach was a dangerous place.

'Are you all right, Matz?' he called, pressing his throat mike.

'I went on the crash course, sir,' Matz answered cheerfully enough, although the prospect before him would have daunted the most experienced tank driver.

'All right, roll 'em!'

Matz pressed his starter. The tank's engines burst into life at once. The roar echoed and re-echoed back and forth. Von Dodenburg glared at the heights to his right. They were empty; then he concentrated on the task ahead, as Matz slipped out the clutch and the Mark IV began squeaking forward in low gear. Behind him the rest of the column followed.

The going was difficult, very difficult. In that confined space there was no leeway for even a fraction of an error. One slip to the left, the slightest skid, the merest extra pressure on the tracks and the 25-ton tank would hurtle over the side into space. In spite of the dawn cold, von Dodenburg found himself sweating furiously.

But the little driver seemed to have ice-water in his veins. Listening over the intercom, von Dodenburg could hear Matz's breath coming at steady regular intervals; he wasn't even cursing as was his wont when the driving became difficult. Matz was concentrating every ounce of alertness he could summon up on the task in hand.

Metre by metre the metal monster clambered up the steep track. In the turret, Schulze and von Dodenburg cocked their ears anxiously to one side, listening urgently for the first sound of cracking shale or any sign of slipping which would carry them over the side. But none came. The tank crawled on.

Now they were totally boxed in, perhaps some fifty metres away from the summit beyond which lay the Ascent. Silently, not daring to disturb Matz's total concentration on the job of driving, von Dodenburg nodded to Schulze. The big NCO understood. They had discussed it the night before. He raised machine pistol and leaned back, levelled it at the towering height above him. On the left of the turret, von Dodenburg did the same, aiming his machine pistol at the edge of the track, as if he half expected some enemy or other to appear over the side at any moment.

★ ★ ★

'Here they come, Englishman,' the Blue Veil Chief hissed, raising his head from the ground, 'I can hear them.' Slaughter could not hear a thing, but then he did not have the phenomenal hearing of the desert Arabs. He nodded to Youssaf, the 16-year-old Blue Veil who had become his lover during the midday break they had taken the day before after three days and nights without sleep. Shyly the handsome boy with his fluttering, coalblack eye-lashes touched Slaughter's hand and then the two of them ran towards the gap in the rocks to the right of the spot where the uphill track ran into the Ascent. All around them, the Blue Veils did the same, merging and disappearing into the surroundings in a flash. Slaughter raised his

Tommy gun, while the boy prepared his ancient, curved-butt rifle. They would fight together – and if necessary die together – as was the custom of the Blue Veils. Up front the aged Chief took one last look at his men's positions and apparently satisfied, ducked into a hole himself. The trap was well and truly set.

* * *

The big tank breasted the rise. Instantly von Dodenburg saw the danger – small round depressions in the sand to their front. '*Stop!*' he yelled desperately.

Matz had seen them only a fraction of a second after the Major and realized too what they were. He braked furiously, The tracks locked. Tearing up sand, rock, scrub, the tank shot down the incline with Matz fighting it frantically to a stop. He managed it. It came to a halt with its front sprockets hanging over the edge of the drop.

The next vehicle – the truck laden with supplies, driven by the Italians – was not so successful. The little Sicilian driver ran straight into the line of mines. There was a tremendous explosion. Its front axle shattered, the driver slumped over the wheel behind the gleaming spider's web of the smashed windscreen, the big truck went plunging down the escarpment, completely out of control. Halfway down it struck an outcrop and went sailing high into the air, somersaulting to the bottom in a fantastic avalanche of sand, rock and bodies. With a great crash it disintegrated there.

Von Dodenburg had no time for the unfortunate Italians. Behind him on the trail, the long line of vehicles had ground to a confused halt and tankers were running up to the top to find out what was the trouble. Von Dodenburg cupped his hands around his mouth and yelled 'Get back…*for God's sake, get back there!*' But even as he spoke, the Blue Veils sprang up from their hiding places and from the steep rock face to the left of the trail. A trooper went down, clutching his stomach. Another clapped his hand to his shoulder with a yelp of pain, swung round by the violence of the slug's impact. Another slapped the ground face-forwards without a sound. Then they broke and fled for the cover of the tanks. The Arabs had them completely pinned down, unable to use their big cannon because they were boxed in by the rocks and the narrow trail. Now it was man against man.

Von Dodenburg and Schulze reacted swiftly. As the first Blue Veils came running towards them, firing from the hip as they did so, the two SS men crouched behind the turret, and loosed a quick burst from left to right. The first wave of the Blue Veils were scythed down in an instant. The next wave suffered the same fate. But the third pushed home their attack boldly. Slugs whined and careered off the tank's armour. The first grenade sailed through the air and landed on the steep glacis plate, rolled off and exploded directly in front of the driver's compartment. 'Sod this for a lark!' Matz cried, '*get me out of here!*'

But the two desperate men on the turret had no time for Matz. The Arabs were swarming all around the tank now. It needed only one well-aimed grenade inside the turret and the slaughter would be complete. Even the 'Prof' seemed to realize that fact. Just as the first Arab poked his cruel face over the top of the turret, he closed his eyes and jerked the trigger of his pistol. The bullet hit the Blue Veil directly in the face at two metres' range. His skull exploded. Shreds of gore and shattered bone flew high in the air and the headless body slumped dead on the armour.

Swearing furiously, an enraged Schulze risked his neck. Raising his body above the cover of the turret, he fired his machine pistol in furious bursts from left to right, sweeping the other Arabs from the tank like flies. Next instant he ducked hastily as a hand grenade exploded on the side of the turret sending shards of red-hot metal howling frighteningly in every direction.

For a moment the Blue Veils held back from attacking. However, elsewhere the snap and crackle of small arms fire indicated that they were still coining forward. Von Dodenburg wiped the sweat from his brow, slammed a new magazine into his Schmeisser and dropped it inside to Matz. 'How are you fixed for mags?' he asked Schulze 'Just one left sir,' Schulze replied. 'I got carried away a minute ago. Wasted too many slugs, I'm afraid.' Von Dodenburg nodded his comprehension and took out his pistol. He had a full magazine in it – nine bullets in all. It was ironic. Here they were in one of the world's most powerful tanks, armed with a 75mm gun and two 7.92mm machine-guns, packed with ammunition, which they were unable to use because the Blue Veils had already crept too close; they simply couldn't depress the guns that low.

'I wonder where that one-eyed arsehole, Doerr has got to?' Schulze asked, slapping the machine pistol's magazine to check that it was fixed correctly.

The thick crump of a grenade shattered against the side of the trapped tank cut brutally into Schulze's words. 'Stand by', von Dodenburg yelled. 'Here they come again!'

The turret armour sang and whined with the slap of slugs ricocheting off it. An Arab loomed up at the back of the turret. The 'Prof' fired and missed. The butt of the Arab's rifle slammed into the elderly academic's face. He crashed back against the armour, his false teeth hanging out of his shattered, bloody mouth.

Schulze spun round. There was no room to use his Schmeisser. He dropped it on the floor and thrusting out his right hand, fingers extended stiffly, poked two of them through the man's veil and into his nostrils. 'Try that one on for size you bloody queer!' he grunted and heaved upwards. The Arab screamed shrilly. Hot blood spurted out of his nostrils and soaked his veil red. Schulze had no pity. He did not relax his terrible grip. Instead he ripped upwards even more, with the Arab wriggling frantically on his fingers like a hooked fish, blood streaming everywhere.

'Look out, Major!' the 'Prof' quavered through bloody, toothless lips.

Von Dodenburg spun round. Two Arabs had appeared above the edge of the turret behind him. He fired instinctively. The right one threw up his arms with a scream of sheer agony and disappeared. The other lunged at the Major with a curved knife. He pressed the trigger of his pistol but nothing happened. He had run out of ammunition! The Arab's dark eyes above the veil sparkled with cruel triumph. His knife whizzed through the air. Just in time von Dodenburg parried it with his pistol. Steel locked against steel. Desperately von Dodenburg pulled back his pistol. Before the Arab could lunge again, he thrashed the pistol across his face. The man's nosebone snapped like a twig underfoot in a dry summer. Great gobs of thick red blood spattered the front of von Dodenburg's shirt. The Arab disappeared over the side of the turret, screaming.

The next moment another appeared, just as Schulze let go of the man he was holding. He dived for his machine pistol. On the turret-edge, the Arab levelled his rifle at the bending man's broad back, a look of triumphant anticipation in his night-black eyes. His finger crooked round the trigger. At that range he couldn't miss.

Just as he fired, a furious burst of 9mm slugs ripped his back away, and hands fluttering frenetically, he fell down to the sand. Von Dodenburg slumped to the bloody, cartridge-case littered metal deck in exhausted relief. There was no mistaking that sound. It was the high-pitched, hysterical hiss of a German machine pistol. Sergeant Doerr had found his way through the rock ridges after all. They were saved!

* * *

'*No!*' the boy warned, as Slaughter raised his Tommy gun to tackle the panzer grenadiers who had appeared on the scene so dramatically and who were now pouring down the slope, firing from the hip at the completely surprised Blue Veils. 'Don't fire!'

Before Slaughter could react, the boy had knocked the Tommy gun from his hands and throwing away his own precious rifle, had raised his hands in a token of surrender.

The nearest panzer grenadier, a fresh-faced youth, eyes wild under his peaked cap, raised his Schmeisser as if to mow the surrendering Blue Veil down. Then he thought better of it. 'All right, keep those paws in the air,' he cried in German, 'and walk up to the halftracks – slowly.'

The Blue Veil did not understand German, but the iron butt of the Schmeisser slamming into his skinny ribs told him all he wanted to know. Hands raised high in the air and accompanied by Slaughter, who had understood the German, he walked up the slope towards the waiting halftracks, their engines still ticking over. 'Can you drive?' the boy asked out of the corner of his mouth, 'one of those?'

Slaughter stepped over the body of the old Chief, his face now looking as if someone had thrown a handful of strawberry jam into it. 'Yes,' he whispered back. 'But what are you going to do?'

Before the boy had time to reply, they were level with the first halftrack and its driver was indicating that they should come forward slowly and be searched, his pistol held at the ready.

The boy advanced as ordered, hands held straight in the air. Behind him, Slaughter gasped. The boy had one of the Blue Veils' tiny, yet deadly throwing knives tied to the back of his wrist by a piece of rag, and the soldier could not see it.

'That's enough,' the young panzer grenadier ordered and jerked his pistol upwards threateningly.

The boy halted. '*NOW!*' he yelled at the top of his voice. He flipped the knife out of its hiding place and in one and the same movement threw it at the startled German. He screamed as it struck him directly in the chest. His legs started to crumple beneath him like those of a new-born foal. The boy kicked him in the crutch to hasten his fall and jumped forward. Slaughter dived after him. A wild burst of fire stitched the sand where they had just been standing. Slaughter flung himself into the driving seat and ripped off the brake. Machine-gun fire shattered the windscreen in front of him. The boy kicked a space clear. Slaughter thrust home first gear and grabbed the wheel. The halftrack slithered and then gripped. Zigzagging crazily, followed by angry cries and a wild hail of bullets, the Englishman steered the halftrack down the Ascent, trailing a billowing plume of sand behind him. With a bone-jarring jolt they hit the bottom and then they were off at top speed, the armour-plating rattling madly, heading east into the desert. Within minutes they were a tiny dot on the horizon. Then they vanished altogether. Slaughter had got away.

THREE

It was nearly thirty-six hours later. Now they were rolling due east. The going was becoming better by the hour and here and there von Dodenburg, standing next to a swollen-mouthed, puckered-lipped Professor, could see the faded tracks of other vehicles in the sand. He knew that they were slowly approaching the Ain Dalla Oasis where they would meet their unknown Egyptian contact.

That day he allowed the crews to have a two hour midday break, although they had overcome their previous exhaustion. The successful outcome of the battle against the Blue Veils had been the tonic they had needed. All the same von Dodenburg insisted that the cooks should prepare a proper meal for them instead of the usual fried sausages or bully beef, and ordered that an extra ration of water should be handed out too. They had overcome the perils of the desert, but ahead of them there was probably an even more perilous venture.

After the meal, while the men lolled or slept in the shade of their vehicles, he called the two young officers and Reichert and Schulze to his command tank. He offered each of them a half-mug of his precious bottle of cognac, then got down to business. 'Now I am sure you have wondered why we have driven so far into this miserable wilderness. Some time I have wondered myself,' he grinned ruefully at them. 'Well, now I can tell you a little about our mission.'

In spite of the terrible heat, the others leaned forward eagerly to listen to their CO's disclosures.

'Within one day's march of here, there is the oasis of Ain Dalla, the furthest British outpost in Egypt. Now, according to my information that outpost is held mainly by men of the Egyptian Army, with only a handful of British present. Am I not right, Prof?' The academic, embarrassed by his lack of teeth contented himself with a quick nod.

'Now,' von Dodenburg continued, 'those Egyptian soldiers are loyal to the German cause, they only need the word from us and they will rise against the British. The Oasis will be in our hands.'

'Holy strawsack!' Meier cried with youthful enthusiasm. 'Imagine – a German base right in the rear of the British Army in Egypt!'

'Just imagine!' Major von Dodenburg agreed, concealing his irony and not attempting to enlighten the bright-eyed boy. There would be time enough to tell him Wotan's real mission later. 'Now I intend to get word to those Egyptians tonight. Both of you young men have proved that you are capable of looking after yourselves and your men, so tonight I'm going to leave you in charge of the column.'

The two officers beamed with pleasure at the CO's praise. Von Dodenburg smiled at them and went on. 'Mind you, you must not be careless, because I'm taking Sergeant Doerr's panzer grenadiers with me. You'll have to flesh out an infantry guard from your crews.'

'Don't worry, sir,' Meier said promptly. 'We'll cope all right, though speaking for myself, I'd prefer to be coming with you towards the sound of the guns.'

'*Sound of my arse!*' Schulze snorted in disgust.

'Shut up, you oaf,' von Dodenburg snapped 'You'll get plenty of action before this business is over, Meier. Never fear. Now I want you to keep radio silence from now onwards. For all I know the Tommies might have a radio detection station at the Oasis and I don't want to give our presence away prematurely. At the same time, I want you to keep a strict radio watch throughout the night. Once we have sorted out the Oasis, I shall signal you. You will come straightaway.'

'*Natürlich!*' the officers agreed in one voice.

'Good, then that's that,' von Dodenburg concluded, rising to his feet.

'And what about me?' Schulze asked.

'You?' von Dodenburg beamed at him maliciously. 'You, you big rogue, are coming with me.'

'Balls of fire!' Schulze cursed. 'Here we go again…'

* * *

They crouched at the edge of the Oasis, shivering in the night cold and nibbling the small dates they had plucked from the trees, watching the flickering fires go out one by one. Next to von Dodenburg, Schulze and Doerr were guzzling the cold spring water as if it was Wotan's favourite *Holsten Bier* from Hamburg.

Von Dodenburg neither ate nor drank. His whole attention was concentrated on the little camp in the centre of Ain Dalla Oasis. He guessed the white bell tents arranged in two rigidly straight lines beneath the palms housed the Tommies. Unlike the average German soldier, the Tommy was highly disciplined and stuck strictly to Army regulations. On the other hand, the shabby, dirty-white pup tents slung haphazardly to the trees, or in patches of camel-grass would belong to the soldiers of the Egyptian Army. Indeed he had seen a fat soldier in khaki with the red fez of an officer on his head go into one of the pup tents before the camp settled down for the night.

Now he plotted the Egyptian sentries' positions, which was not difficult; the Egyptians were very careless, lighting cigarettes and calling to each other in alarm whenever they were startled by the mysterious night noises Of the desert. In all there were six of them: two in the centre of the Oasis and four others patrolling the extremities. It would not be difficult to nobble them, he told himself, before they could raise the alarm.

He rolled over on his stomach and faced Schulze. 'Listen, you and I are going down there.'

Schulze clenched his ham of a fist. 'Gonna get us a couple of those nig-nogs are we, sir?' he asked in happy anticipation.

'No, we are not, Schulze. We're just going to nobble one of their sentries before he can call out. But I don't want him injured. I want him in good shape so that he can tell us who's in charge down there and how he's going to deal with the Tommies. Clear?'

'Clear, sir.'

Von Dodenburg turned to Doerr. 'Sergeant, stand by with your panzer grenadiers. If we run into trouble, I'll fire a red and green flare. Then you come running.'

'Yes sir,' Doerr rapped smartly, and nudged Schulze. 'Keep a tight asshole, Schulzi!'

Swiftly they slipped into the trees, heading towards the sentry on the nearside of the oasis. In an instant they had vanished into the pre-dawn gloom.

From their position in the dusty rocks near the bubbling spring the two SS men could see every detail of the sleeping sentry's face, as he dozed at his post, his back against one of the palms. He had a thin, stupid face and von Dodenburg knew that if he spotted them his first reaction would be one of fear; he would cry out.

He clapped his hands over Schulze's ear. 'Work round the back of him. No noise. I don't want him yelling his head off. I'll come in from the front.'

Schulze nodded his understanding. At once he wormed his way into the lush undergrowth around the spring and started to come in from the rear. Von Dodenburg crawled forward on his hands and knees, taking his time, his eyes intent on the sentry.

The sentry stirred. He had heard the faint noise the crawling officer was making. His eyelids flickered. Slowly he began to open his eyes. Von Dodenburg tensed. The sentry saw him. He opened his mouth to scream, just as von Dodenburg had anticipated he would, in the same instant that Schulze's brawny arm reached round the back of the palm tree and hooked around the sentry's skinny neck, smothering the cry.

Hastily von Dodenburg rose to his feet and faced the terrified Egyptian. 'Listen,' he said in hesitant English. 'No one will hurt you. We are friends. Do you understand?' He nodded to Schulze and the NCO relaxed his grip sufficiently so that the man could answer.

Nothing came. The Egyptian's dark eyes rolled in wild fear – that was all. He did not understand English.

Von Dodenburg tried German, knowing as he did so that it was hardly likely that this product of some Cairo slum would be able to understand him. He was right. All that the man's eyes registered was blank, naked fear.

He had not calculated that the only language the man would understand would be his own. 'All right, Schulze,' he decided swiftly, 'let's get him back. The Prof will have to explain everything to him in his own lingo. Come on – quick!'

★ ★ ★

'His CO's name is Salah Mustafa – Major Mustafa,' the 'Prof' translated the sentry's words, as he squatted there, still a little fearful, in the middle of the crouched panzer grenadiers.

'Ask him if he likes the English?' von Dodenburg commanded. The Egyptian's dark eyes blazed fanatically in response to this question and he drew his skinny brown forefinger across his throat as if he were slitting it open with a knife-blade.

'Have they a radio station at the Oasis?' was von Dodenburg's next question.

The Egyptian answered that the British had one and they kept it exclusively under their control. Major Mustafa's Egyptians were not allowed to use it.

Von Dodenburg checked his watch. In another thirty minutes it would be dawn and the Tommies undoubtedly would get up. Everyone rose early in the desert, even the English. He would have to act – and act quickly.

Keeping his eyes fixed on the sentry's skinny face, he said: 'Prof, tell him this – and make it simple and clear. He must wake his Major and tell him the Germans are coming in – in exactly thirty minutes. It will be the Major's task to ensure that the Tommies do not get to that radio set before we move in. All right?'

With much gesticulation, accompanied by excited nodding on the part of the sentry, the 'Prof' translated von Dodenburg's words.

A few moments later he was gone, scuttling through the still palm trees to pass on von Dodenburg's message to his commander.

Hurriedly von Dodenburg made his own preparations for the attack. The panzer grenadiers would go in from both sides. There was to be no firing until they reached the white bell tents. That way there would be no risk of their new allies being hurt. Both groups would rendezvous on the radio tent, easily identifiable by the twin radio masts attached to its exterior.

'Remember no firing at all unless the Tommies put up any sort of resistance,' were von Dodenburg's last words and with that the panzer grenadiers dispersed to their start positions, the new recruits among them clutching their weapons nervously in suddenly damp hands.

★ ★ ★

But there was to be no combat for Sergeant Doerr's panzer grenadiers that dawn. Five minutes before zero hour, von Dodenburg, crouching in the undergrowth with Schulze and the 'Prof', was startled by a sudden burst of machine-gun fire followed by a series of screams. He rose to his feet at once and blew his whistle shrilly. 'Come in,' he called and charged forward at the head of the other section of panzer grenadiers.

Their sudden rush came to a halt among the tents. Tommies, most of them naked or clad only in their underpants were lying slaughtered as they slept. While the SS men stood there shocked and bewildered, a group of grinning Egyptian soldiers butchered a grievously wounded Tommy, plunging their long bayonets time and time again into his naked back with wolfish pleasure. The tented camp was a bloody hell of murdered men, scuffed sand, gleaming empty cartridge cases, the groans of the dying drowned by the excited cries of the Egyptians who were already looting the possessions of the men whom they had just murdered. It was too much, even for hard-bitten Sergeant Doerr. He kicked the Egyptians plunging their bayonets into the body of the British soldier and shouted, 'Stop it, you bunch of treacherous bastards!'

Von Dodenburg pulled him away just as the Egyptians' commanding officer appeared from behind the radio tent.

'Major Mustafa, at your service!' he announced and raised his flabby hand to his jauntily tilted red fez, flashing von Dodenburg a gold-toothed smile. 'We have done our job well – no?'

Von Dodenburg looked at the Major's pale face adorned with an immense pair of dyed black moustaches in a ludicrous imitation of a British Army officer, and took an instant dislike to the man. All the same he saluted and said: 'You have done an excellent job, Major. Let me introduce myself. Von Dodenburg, Major, SS Battalion Wotan.'

'Charmed,' Major Mustafa said and extended his hand.

Von Dodenburg took it. The hand was flabby, damp and disgusting. He swore to himself that he would not touch another person until he had washed his own hand. 'Did you get the radio station, Major?' he asked urgently.

Again the Major flashed that brilliant smile and indicated the young Tommy lying naked in the sand, a bayonet protruding from between his shoulder blades and what looked like a carving knife skewered right through his left leg and deep into the sand. 'Yes, the pig didn't want to die.'

'The radio operator?'

'Exactly,' the Major smirked. 'We of the Royal Egyptian Army are matched only by your own Army in efficiency.' His smile vanished and he looked around the handful of panzer grenadiers grouped among the tents. 'But is this all that his Excellency Marshal Rommel has sent us to rouse the Delta?' he asked in sudden alarm.

Von Dodenburg shook his head and fought back his disgust; he had seen the sudden look of abject fear in the Egyptian's black eyes. 'No, I have a full company of tanks out there in the desert, waiting for my signal… Mark IVs,' he added.

'Mark IVs!' the Major breathed, his fear vanishing immediately. 'Excellent, the most powerful tank in the desert. Now we shall show those pigs of Englishmen.'

He spat viciously into the sand.

'How?' von Dodenburg protested. 'I don't even know who my

contact is for the next stage of this operation.'

The Major smiled. 'Be patient, my dear Major. We patriots have to be careful – very careful. The English have their spies everywhere in Egypt. As soon as my chaps have cleared away the mess in the radio tent, I shall personally raise our contact in Alexandria. No doubt, she will be here within twenty-four hours to give you full instructions.'

'She!' von Dodenburg exclaimed.

'Yes,' the Egyptian answered with a fat smile of pleasure. 'Madame is the bravest of the brave. Not even Nassar and Sadat surpass her in courage and hatred of the English.' He touched his swagger stick to his fez jauntily. 'Now you must excuse me, Major, I must see that this rubbish' – he kicked the young radio operator's dead body – 'is cleared away.' He left von Dodenburg staring at his fat back in disbelief.

Madame! Now he knew why Field-Marshal Rommel had laughed when he had told him about his contact. Von Dodenburg shook his head, like a man trying to wake from a heavy sleep. What had he let himself in for with this comic opera mob – what indeed…?

SECTION FOUR:

A BATTLE IS PROPOSED

'Now this is the form. There must be no more failures. The men have experienced too many of them – they will tolerate no more.'

General Montgomery to his Staff, El Alamein

ONE

'You will please extinguish your cigarettes – and you will have exactly thirty seconds to cough. Thereafter there will be no more noise,' the undersized, birdlike Commander announced, having, as always, a little difficulty with the pronunciation of his 'r's.

Dutifully the staff officers assembled outside his caravan stubbed out their cigarettes and cleared their throats. While the new commander of the Eighth Army spoke, they knew it would be fatal to cough. As they knew from the reports coming in from the U.K. about him, he had already pitched a full divisional commander out of a briefing for doing exactly that.

General Montgomery beamed at them intently. 'Good,' he said and tapped the big map pinned on the blackboard next to him. 'Now, chaps, this is the form. The Battle of Alam Halfa last month delayed my own offensive. But if we'd have lost it, we would have lost Egypt to the Hun. Besides it was a boost for the Eighth Army and has given Tommy Atkins new confidence in the Command, which was sadly lacking in the past.' He stared around at their faces, which were bronzed unlike his own, which was still white from an English winter. Some of the staff officers lowered their eyes, as if they were embarrassed by their commanders' past failures.

Montgomery raised his voice. 'Well, chaps, Alam Halfa is history. We are concerned with the future, eh? How are we going to knock Jerry for a six – and for good. That's the problem?' He tapped the map. 'The basic problem that confronts us is a difficult one. We face

Rommel between the sea and the Qattara Depression on a front of forty-five miles. Intelligence tells me that Rommel is strengthening his defensive positions to a depth previously unknown in the desert. In addition there is no open or easy flank for us to go through or turn. In essence, gentlemen, it is going to be a slogging match.'

He let the information sink in before continuing 'I'm sure that Rommel is expecting us. It is impossible to conceal the fact that we are going to launch an attack. The best we can do is to achieve tactical surprise. Our deception experts are working on it

The staff officers looked knowingly at one another. What effective deception could Montgomery's 'experts' carry out in the completely open desert? All the same the cocky General seemed supremely confident and that was new in 8th Army commanders.

If the new Commander saw their looks, he did not let himself be affected by them; he continued his exposé in the same self-assured manner as before. 'Now, we'll need a full moon to launch this one. The chaps will need to see their way through the Jerry minefields. Can't have a waning moon. Why you may ask? Because I envisage a real dog-fight for about a week before we can break out and we'll need all the light we can get at night. So, gentlemen, you can guess when we're going to attack.' He looked challengingly around his listeners' faces like a keen schoolmaster, expecting the best from his brighter pupils. 'Yes, Horrocks?' he demanded of the long-faced, silver-haired commander of his XIII Corps.

'About the end of October?' General Horrocks ventured.

Montgomery beamed. 'Exactly! According to the Met people, twenty-third of October to be completely precise, with full moon on the twenty-fourth. When do

we attack then, chaps? I shall tell you. On the night of the twenty-third, just to keep Rommel on the hop.

Montgomery waited till the excited buzz of chatter had died away before he spoke again. 'Now this is the form,' he said and this time the thin smile on his lips had vanished and there was iron in his voice. 'There must be no more failures. The men have experienced too many of them – they will tolerate no more. The people back home want victory, too. They have suffered nothing but defeats these last three black years. And, gentlemen, *I want victory!* Because my reputation depends upon it.' Montgomery said the words without a trace of embarrassment and his audience was amazed. Didn't he know that Rommel had beaten British commander after commander, smashed attack after attack, destroyed plan after plan? The Desert Fox always had some sort of trick up his sleeve. Would he not be able to turn the tables on this cocky little commander in the Tank Corps beret, who stood before them so bravely this burningly hot morning?

Montgomery seemed to be able to read their thoughts. He chuckled, a strange sound from a man who had so slight a sense of humour. 'You think you've heard it all before – from the generals who preceded me, gentlemen, don't you? Perhaps you have. But those gentlemen were not Bernard Montgomery. This time Rommel will not fool me.' He turned as if he were about to go into his caravan again. Then he seemed to change his mind. Facing them once more, he said: 'Let me tell you one last thing – in confidence – gentlemen. For the first two days or so of the battle I will not be fighting General Rommel. I shall be fighting his deputy, General Stumme. Rommel is on sick leave in Germany. Naturally he will hurry back once the battle starts, but by that time poor General Stumme will have lost it and I shall be the victor.' He touched his hand to his beret very casually, pleased with the impact of this news. 'Good morning. Thank you, gentlemen, that is all.'

'Christ Almighty,' a flabbergasted staff officer whispered to General Horrocks, after Montgomery had disappeared inside, 'who the devil does he think he is – *God!*'

'No,' General Horrocks replied urbanely, 'Jesus Christ would be my guess...'

TWO

If General Montgomery was confident that he was to be the victor of the impending battle, the few British and the many Egyptians of Delta's second largest city, Alexandria, were definitely not. Their money was on a German breakthrough.

A ragged Slaughter, accompanied by the wide-eyed boy could see that Alex was in a flap. There were middle-class Egyptians and British Army staff wallahs packing up and leaving the endangered city everywhere, jeered at by the ragged Egyptian poor who lined the streets. Once a portly British colonel, with the red tabs of the staff on his jacket, accompanied by his young blonde mistress, pulled up in front of them, halted by a barefoot policeman on point-duty. The skinny onlookers jeered and spat at the car. Pointing at the city's scavengers, the brown kites sailing lazily above them in the still air, they cried: 'They're waiting for you, fat Englishman, when the Germans come!

Richer Egyptians were flooding westwards in a slow moving mass of traffic, which grew even denser as the day wore on. Their cars were crammed with suitcases

and shapeless bundles, and almost invariably topped by a canopy of striped mattresses tied on with scraps of rope as protection against aerial attacks. Over all the sweating, slow-moving column there hung an atmosphere of latent terror.

The boy looked at the Egyptians in wonder. Slaughter nudged him and said with contempt, 'There are two species of men in the

Delta, boy. The great mass of the fellaheen, miserable human scavengers – and those men you see in the motor cars: the masters. They smell of perfume and corruption – *and fear!*' He spat in the dust. The two of them came in sight of the great barracks. In the whorehouses ringing the place the half-naked whores hung out of the windows jeering at the glum-faced soldiers and singing mockingly:

'Me no likee English sold-ier

Ger-man soldier come ashore

Ger-man soldier plenty mon-ey

Me no jigajag for you no more.'

This time Slaughter did not attempt to steal into Mustafa Barracks. He had no time. Instead he showed his pass and was allowed through immediately, followed by the boy. They passed a pile of secret documents being burnt on the parade ground under the supervision of grim-faced Redcaps. Obviously Mustafa Barracks was preparing for the worst.

* * *

Five minutes in the echoing anteroom opposite Brigadier Young's office told Slaughter that the base wallahs had little confidence in the new Commander's ability to win the impending battle. Immaculate staff officers hurried to and fro with anxious drawn faces, speaking in grave whispers, and from behind one of the closed office doors, he could hear a petulant upper-class voice saying: 'But it is as clear as the nose on your face, old chap. The wogs are ready to rise up at any moment. There'll be blood in the streets before this week is out. Believe you me.'

Finally Brigadier Young was ready to receive him. Slaughter strode into the big airless room. Young looked much older than when he had last seen him. There were dark blue circles under his eyes and there was a nervous tic in his left cheek which he seemed unable to control.

'Good to see you again, Slaughter,' he said without conviction, his voice slightly unsteady, 'and your news?'

'The Jerries have broken through the Great Sano Sea. My boys and I failed to stop them at the Ascent. For all I know they are now heading for the coast.'

Brigadier Young looked at the ragged little Intelligence man aghast. 'Oh, my God,' he groaned. 'How many, in heaven's name?'

'Perhaps a couple of hundred of them, at the most, sir. But I counted at least a dozen Mark IVs.'

'Christ! Not even the new Sherman can stand up to that monster.' Young stopped and thought for a moment. 'But I say, Slaughter,' he said, a little more cheerfully, 'a company or two of Jerry infantry, even if they are supported by tanks, can't do that much, can they?'

'I'm afraid they can!' Slaughter said severely. There were too many officers in the Delta like Brigadier Young, who invariably misread the situation in Egypt. One day, if they weren't careful, they'd lose not only Egypt but the whole of the Middle East because of it.

'As far as the Gippos are concerned, the Germans are simply cannon-fodder. They are expendable. But let them appear in Cairo or here in Alex and be shot to pieces by our chaps, and they'll be the symbol the plotters need to rouse the students and fellaheen. Thereafter the Germans can disappear from the scene.' He pressed home his point brutally. 'Let that armour appear in the centre of Cairo – and it's my guess that is where they are heading – for one single hour, and we'll have a revolution on our hands. The Eighth will be stabbed in the back and, within a week, Rommel will be on the Nile.'

Brigadier Young gave a groan and let his greying head sink into his hands in a gesture of utter defeat. 'What can we do? *My God, what can we do?*' he gasped. Suddenly his body was racked by a sob.

Slaughter looked at the Brigadier's heaving shoulders with contempt. He and his boys had more guts than all these big tough he-men, who broke down like women once real trouble started.

'What can we do?' he echoed, iron in his voice. 'This is what *you* can do. You can give me the forty odd SAS men you still have here at Mustafa.'

Brigadier Young raised his head slowly. 'But what good are a couple of score men, even if they are from the Special Air Service?' he asked in a voice thick with emotion.

Slaughter leaned forward across the big desk and told him in an urgent flow of words. When he was finished, he looked eagerly at the Brigadier. 'Well, sir, what do you think?'

'But my God, Slaughter,' Young protested. 'I'm a British officer, you're a British officer. We can't condone – *murder!*'

Slaughter's eyes blazed. 'Listen, Young,' he snarled, dropping all pretence of military courtesy. 'If we lose the British Empire, it will be because of people like you. Our forefathers – the men who gained the Empire for us – were ruthless, brutal, unscrupulous thieves and murderers, whose sole morality was – what is good for England is good. This time if the Germans break though the Delta, they will undoubtedly capture the Suez Canal. When that goes there'll be nothing to stop them until they reach India and you know what desperate straits we are in there due to Jap pressure. Failure this time could well mean the end of the British Empire.'

'*The end of the British Empire!*' Young breathed.

'Yes.' Slaughter pressed home his point, forcing a smile although he had never felt less like smiling in all his life. 'Look at it this way, sir. One day we'll order another Scotch in some London pub and paint up this bitch of a war in such wondrous colours that she'll look like a latterday saint. The real, nasty bitch will be forgotten. But first we've got to win it! Then what we *have* to do this month no-one will want to remember.' Slaughter's fake smile vanished. 'Do I get those SAS men, sir?'

Brigadier Young gave in. With a hand that shook, he picked up his bell. 'You get them, Slaughter.... But for God's sake, never let me see your face in this office again...'

THREE

The SAS man's big ammo boot crashed against the door. The wood around the lock splintered and gave and they moved in. Two of them, with Slaughter bringing up the rear, crashed into the hail, slithering on the tiled floor. From upstairs there were cries of alarm. A woman shouted something in Arabic. When there was no answer she repeated her demand in atrocious French.

Slaughter nodded. The two big SAS men raced up the marble steps. From above there came the sound of cries, blows, and curses. 'Is this him, sir?' the SAS Corporal demanded, thrusting their prisoner to the edge of the decorative iron-work.

Slaughter stared up at the trembling face of the man in the striped lounging pyjamas, which the richer Egyptians liked to wear in the afternoon. 'That's him,' he snapped. The Egyptian politician seemed suddenly to realize what they were going to do. 'No, no, please,' he cried in English. 'I have wife, I have children. *No...no...*' His pleas ended in a howl of pain as the other SAS man rammed the butt of his sten onto his fat brown fingers, clinging desperately to the rail. The next moment the two of them seized him and tossed him down into the hall below. He screamed and hit the marble floor like a sack of wet cement. His spine snapped audibly and his head twisted at an impossible angle. Slaughter knelt down swiftly, while the two SAS men clattered down the stairs. 'Dead,' he announced.

'Come on,' the big Corporal said. 'Let's beat it before the Gippo rozzers turn up!'

They ran out of the open door, leaving behind the silence of death.

* * *

'*But I am a doctor*,' the Egyptian protested across the metal table, littered with gleaming instruments of his calling. 'I am not interested in politics. None of us here is interested in politics, simply in medicine.'

Hastily Slaughter checked his list. 'You are all traitors and terrorists,' he announced. 'You, Dr Ali Hamshari, Dr Abdel Shibi and Dr Mustafa Hafez.'

The young bespectacled Egyptian doctor knew he was trapped. The clinic was packed with illegal explosives and by now the British rummaging around below must have found them. 'We are patriots,' he declared proudly, 'whose sole aim is to throw you English out of our –'

A SAS man rammed his rifle butt into the doctor's stomach and his words ended in a startled gasp of pain. 'Outside with them,' Slaughter ordered, putting away his list till the next house, '*shoot 'em!*'

* * *

The Egyptian, whose playboy image had concealed his work for the revolution, suddenly jabbed his elbow into the stomach of the SAS man holding him, while Slaughter checked his list. The SAS was caught off guard and the Egyptian dived for the door.

The SAS corporal was quicker. He fired from the hip. The luxurious penthouse apartment stank of cordite and the fugitive screamed and dropped to the thickly carpeted floor. Blood pouring from the gaping hole in his back and dripping onto the white sheepskin carpet, he continued to crawl to the door.

Slaughter nodded to the boy, whose eyes gleamed. He pulled out his knife and crouching over the crawling man, drew the wicked curved blade across his throat, as if he were slaughtering a sheep. The boy looked up and grinned, he wiped his bloody knife on the Egyptian's immaculate Savile Row suit.

'Miserable bastard,' Slaughter said and ticked the playboy's name off his list. 'Come on, all of you.'

* * *

That afternoon, Slaughter and his hardened SAS carried out their bloody task. Blinded by hatred of the 'gippos' and the 'wogs' and brutalized by their years of hard fighting and hard living in the desert, the troopers under Slaughter's command rushed from house to house all that long October afternoon, murdering those suspected by the Major of belonging to the organization which was ready to rise up and throw the British out of Egypt. Twice they bluffed their way into Egyptian Army barracks and before the eyes of hundreds of Egyptian soldiers, shot down young officers who belonged to the group around Nasser. They told the provost marshal permanently stationed outside Dolly's House, the capital's most expensive brothel, to disappear, and in the heavy luxury of that perfumed place, stabbed the Egyptian General to death, as he lay in the arms of his black girl.

But slowly the plotters in the capital found out what was going on. The telephone lines buzzed with rumours and warnings. Nasser went underground. The King ordered his palace to be locked and shuttered, and called out the Palace Guard. One by one the survivors, so confident that morning that nothing could go wrong with their plan, fled like the rats they were, and as that terrible afternoon drew to a close, Major Slaughter began to feel that he had crushed the revolt before it had really started.

But Major Slaughter was wrong for once. For just before the death of the young Egyptian Army Captain, standing ashen-face with fear in his bedroom, he had the presence of mind to call a number in Alexandria and give her the alternative code-word. She gasped an anxious query.

'Pomme,' he began, just as the Englishmen broke into his bedroom, stens blazing. He went down, his stomach ripped open in a welter of blood and entrails, with her name on his dying lips. '*Pomme…*'

FOUR

The clatter of the tracks alerted the whole oasis. Von Dodenburg, who had been dozing in the shade of a palm tree sprang to his feet in alarm. But Schulze beat him to it. 'All right, you crappy wet-tails,' he bellowed, fumbling furiously for his machine-pistol, 'get the lead out of your asses! We're getting visitors!'

The tankers ran for their vehicles, carefully camouflaged by palm fronds, while the half-naked panzer grenadiers doubled for the slit trenches they had dug all around the oasis.

Von Dodenburg ran across to Major Mustafa's tent. For once the fat Egyptian Major, who seemingly spent most afternoons dallying with his handsome young batman, was not in his bunk. Von Dodenburg had no time to ponder his disappearance. 'Come on, the lot of you,' he yelled to the crew of his command tank. 'Let's see what's going on!'

With the 'Prof' trailing behind, von Dodenburg, Schulze and Matz doubled through the burning sand to where the command tank was hidden at the edge of the northern side of the oasis. Von Dodenburg focused his binoculars on the lone vehicle ploughing its way through the desert.

He had never seen anything like it before. The top seemed to belong to a large civilian car, vintage 1920, or thereabouts, but instead of the wheels one would expect on such a vehicle, they were replaced by tracks.

Swiftly he handed the glasses to Matz. 'What do you make of it, Corporal?' he asked Wotan's vehicle recognition expert.

Matz surveyed the vehicle in silence for a while, as it came ever closer, his leathery face creased in a puzzled frown. 'I don't know exactly, sir. But I think it's a 'twenties Rolls-Royce mounted on probably a Berliet track chassis. The Tommies and the Frogs used them on their trans-Sahara expeditions in the 'thirties.'

Von Dodenburg's face hardened. 'Allies eh?' Blowing three shrill signal blasts on his whistle, he cried: 'Stand by everybody! This might be trouble!'

Throughout the oasis, the camouflaged tanks swung their long hooded guns towards the strange vehicle which seemed to be walkmg straight into their trap. Tensely the half-naked crews waited for the order to fire.

But for once, Wotan's muscle was not needed; for to von Dodenburg's surprise, a familiar figure plodded stolidly into the bright circle of his lenses and approached the slow-moving vehicle. It was the Egyptian Major. As von Dodenburg watched in complete bewilderment, the tracked vehicle stopped. The major clicked to attention and saluted, before crooking his arm around the cab support and waving the unseen driver to proceed. 'Now what the devil is that fat fool up to now?' the Major hissed.

'Let's go and see, sir,' Schulze suggested, already dropping to the ground and waving his arms back and forth to indicate that the gunners should not shoot in anticipation of von Dodenburg's expected order.

Together, followed by Matz and the 'Prof', they thrust their way through the palms towards the strange vehicle, watching the Major busily chatting to the car's passenger, who was still obscured by his body.

With a groan and a hiss of escaping steam from the boiling radiator the ancient conveyance came to a halt. The Major dropped into the sand and with a great flourish opened the squeaky rear door, which they could now see was adorned with an elaborate coat-of-arms containing enough heraldic animals to stock a small zoo.

Schulze caught a glimpse of an elegant, silk-clad leg beyond the Egyptian Major's bulk and nudged Matz excitedly in the ribs. '*Shit!*' he whispered.

'Impossible,' Matz breathed. 'It's a mirage!'

'Shut up!' von Dodenburg began and then his mouth fell open with surprise when he saw the woman who emerged from the back of the ancient Rolls.

She was a small woman, who stepped out of the car like a jewelled bird, all fluttering hands, her bright eyes darting along the faces of the staring soldiers, her raddled cheeks rouged and her dyed canary-yellow hair aglow. 'Hello, boys,' she cried in a husky American voice and waved a hand at them, the fingers of which looked as if they had just been dipped in bright-red blood. 'I must look a sight. My maid didn't have time to arrange my eyelashes in Alex.' She giggled at her own joke, which meant nothing to the gawping German and Egyptian soldiers.

The beaming Egyptian Major turned to von Dodenburg. 'Major,' he said with smirking formality, 'may I present you to your contact from our glorious Movement, Madame —'

The strange woman beat him to it. She extended her skinny, hand to von Dodenburg to be kissed and said: 'They call me Pomme,' she breathed, fluttering her false eyelashes madly, 'because I've been eaten so much, I guess.' And with that she went off into another peal of shrill laughter...

* * *

Sue-Ann 'Appleblossom' Keppel had been born in Austin, Texas. Her voice as a long-distance telephone operator had so charmed a Texas cattle baron that he had made a blind date with her and within the month they were married. Six months later, he was dead — 'She plum screwed him to death,' the neighbours said maliciously — and suddenly she found herself the heiress to a fortune of fifty million dollars.

The widow, clad in black from head to foot, flew immediately to New York, where she dumped the expensive widow's weeds in a hotel room, changed into an outrageous red costume, picked up the first man she found in the hotel bar, went to bed with him for the next forty-eight hours and left for Europe the day afterwards. She bought her way into London society, or that part of it which suited her own tastes – 'dope, drink and niggers', as they were in those years But there were those in London society who felt she was 'common' with her vulgar American accent and her painted face. In 1930 she gave it up and moved to the Riviera, where the local 'set' were more to her own wild taste.

There were naked luncheon parties on board the flat-bottomed boats anchored off their gleaming coastal villas; drunken speed-boat trips; long hours of naked, doped sunbathing; masked balls that invariably ended in an orgy. For half a decade she drifted in drunken, drugged ecstasy through the decadent pleasures of a glamorous society which was doomed to extinction in 1940.

In 1935 she met Ali, an Egyptian who was half her age, a 'simply divine dancer', as she described him to the set. Ali swept her off her feet and when he learned that the middle-aged woman was a multi-millionairess, his ardour increased tenfold. He promised her the Pyramids, the Nile, the Desert. Pomme's romantic imagination, which had been moulded as an adolescent by Ramon Navarro, blossomed. She told the set she was going to Egypt on her 'honeymoon'. When they replied that she was not yet married, she told them that 'Pomme never buys a pig in a poke. You know these Eastern guys – very exotic, but no endurance. We'll get hitched later.'

But the 'honeymoon' on the Nile had never taken place. At Alex the British security police were waiting for Ali. Not only had he stolen five thousand Egyptian pounds from the Cairo bank where he had worked, he had also used half of it to buy weapons for the illegal Egyptian terrorist movement. Ali disappeared behind bars; she never saw him again.

Pomme stayed in Egypt. She discovered that Cairo and Alex were full of 'Alis'. A succession of them comforted her, and her sexual desires were replaced by political ambition. As she told visiting members of the set who wondered why she had buried herself in Egypt: 'Peggy Guggenheim collects paintings. I collect revolutionaries – they're much more stimulating!'

But the slaughter of the Cairo underground movement the previous day had made her realize for the first time in a long life of pleasure that she was in danger – real danger. The game – playing at revolution – was over. Either the Egyptians pulled it off and kicked out the English, or the limeys would throw her into jail. All her money wouldn't save her, she knew that. The English had shown just how cruel, how ruthless they could really be when the chips were down. On this October afternoon in the desert Sue-Ann Keppel was scared!

★ ★ ★

She rapped her hard bony fingers on the table, as if she was wearing tiny ivory thimbles and announced 'Major von Duisburg–'

'Dodenburg,' von Dodenburg corrected her, half amused and half alarmed by this flamboyant woman whose orders he was – apparently – to follow.

'Now there has been serious trouble in Cairo, very serious. The Limeys must have tumbled to what was going on there. All day yesterday, they sent out their killers…' In a hectic, breathless flow of words, she explained the events of the past twenty-four hours in the Egyptian capital, and how Slaughter's murderous methods had crushed the planned revolt in that city. 'Sadat and Nasser,' she said, mentioning names which meant nothing to von Dodenburg, but which earned the fat Egyptian Major's enthusiastic praise, 'have gone underground. We can count them out of what is to come. But the Limeys have not reckoned with yours truly. Pomme managed to get out from under and warn our organization in Alexandria. Our group is still pretty well intact there, and Pomme still has a couple of surprises for the Limeys up her knickers. If she wore any, which she don't!

'Before I discuss any plans, young man,' Pomme went on, 'let's have a drink. My tonsils are shrivelled.'

'Coffee?' von Dodenburg suggested.

'*Coffee!*' she exclaimed in mock horror. 'Coffee is for peasants. I only drink champagne.' She looked up at Schulze, his enormous chest gleaming with sweat. 'Sonny, you go over to my vehicle and get the key from that nigger at the wheel. You'll find a chest of iced champagne in the boot.'

Schulze sprang to attention and bowing stiffly, saluted as if he were a member of the old Prussian *Garde du Corps*. '*Zu Befehl, gnadige Frau*,' he snapped in his best German. Von Dodenburg looked up at him in open disbelief. 'Nice young fellah,' Pomme said slowly and thoughtfully, as Schulze moved out of the shade of the palms to fetch the champagne. 'From the way his shorts grab his crotch, it looks as if he carries a nice cannon around with him.'

Five minutes later, Pomme raised her sparkling glass of pink champagne. 'Well, gents,' she toasted the officers, 'here's mud in your eyes. Down the hatch!' She downed the sparkling wine in one gulp, much to the admiration of a watching Schulze.

'The Limeys think they've got everything nicely wrapped up in the Delta. Well, they might have in Cairo. All the same, old Pomme thinks she can still catch them out.'

'How?' von Dodenburg demanded.

By way of an answer, she thrust her empty glass at Schulze. 'Here, handsome, fill 'em up again,' she said.

Schulze did not understand English, but he understood that particular gesture well enough. He did what she commanded, while von Dodenburg waited impatiently for the woman to answer his question. 'Thanks, handsome,' she looked up at the giant ex-docker. 'I bet you could bring a sparkle to a girl's eyes,' she breathed, fluttering her long false eyelashes in maidenly confusion.

'*Madame Pomme!*' von Dodenburg said firmly.

'Oh, yes, I was saying.' She downed the champagne in one quick gulp. '*Alex! ... Alexandria is the place where we're gonna screw the Limeys!*'

FIVE

Schulze lay exhausted in the palms, next to a disgruntled Matz, watching the departure ceremonies. Idly he soothed the blood-red marks that covered his broad back. 'What a woman,' he breathed, as he followed Pomme's progress to the waiting Rolls, 'what a damn woman!'

'You might have thought of yer old pal, Schulze,' Matz said miserably. 'I haven't had a bit since the House.' Schuize did not take his admiring gaze off the woman, who was now saying a few last words to von Dodenburg at the door of the Rolls. 'You don't share a woman like that, even with your best friend, Matzi,' he replied in a hushed voice. 'That would be almost... almost...' he fumbled for a word to express the depth of his emotion, '...against religion. Sacrilege, I think they call it.'

'Ballocks,' Matz snapped unfeelingly.

Schulze ignored his friend's impassioned outburst. Out in the desert, the coloured driver had started the engine. Von Dodenburg closed the door behind Pomme. The driver engaged first gear and with a rusty squeak of tracks, the Rolls started to move off. Von Dodenburg and the Egyptian Major stiffened to attention and saluted. A white arm appeared through the window and answered their salute with a flutter of a white lace handkerchief.

The Major caught sight of Matz. 'Corporal, where's the other rogue?' he demanded.

'Sergeant Major Schulze?'

'Yes.'

'He's over there in palms, sir.'

'The latrine?' von Dodenburg queried.

'No sir,' Matz answered, completely straight-faced, though there was a malicious gleam in his wicked little eyes, 'I think he's collecting a few flowers – for Madame.'

'You'll have my boot up your flowery arse in a minute, you cheeky rogue,' von Dodenburg snorted. 'Get him over here. I want to assemble the company. I have something to say to them.'

'At the double, sir!' Matz answered smartly. He floundered through the sand to where Schulze still lay dreamily, staring after the black dot of the Rolls.

With a reluctant sigh, Schulze clambered to his feet and cupping his hands to his mouth, he called with unusual mildness: 'All right, you fellows, fall in in the centre of the oasis. The CO wants to have a chat with us.'

Matz shook his head in disbelief. 'As I live and breathe,' he said, '*Schulze's in love!*'

* * *

But Major von Dodenburg's voice, when he spoke to the assembled company, was dry, cold and completely unemotional. Pomme was a bold, resourceful woman and the Egyptian Major had been full of enthusiasm for her plan. But to von Dodenburg it seemed not only 'daring' (as the Egyptian had described it the night before), but decidedly dicey. If it went wrong, the company would be isolated in the middle of a British-held town, hundreds of kilometres away from the nearest German troops.

'Soldiers, comrades,' he began formally, staring at the honest young faces of the boys seated around him. 'At last, I can tell you what the real purpose of our mission here is – why we have had to undertake such a terrible journey through the desert to this God-forsaken place. We are to strike a blow against the enemy in Egypt, which will enable Marshal Rommel to achieve final victory and allow him to throw the Tommies out of Egypt for good – perhaps out of Africa altogether.'

He allowed them a few moments of excited chatter, before holding up his hand for silence. 'As you all realize, a handful of men, even from Assault Regiment Wotan, cannot drive the Tommies from Egypt. We need the aid of the native population to do that, and we must realize that the local people need proof that the Germans will come to their assistance and support them when they rise against the English tyrants.'

'What then is our task, comrades?'

Von Dodenburg answered his own question. 'It is going to be a bold and dangerous one. To the north of this oasis lies Egypt's second largest city. At present, according to the information I have received from our Egyptian allies, it is thinly defended by British troops. They have all been sent to the desert. What is left of them is concentrated in one large military installation – Mustafa Barracks.' He licked his lips, suddenly dry, when he thought of what he was going to have to say next in order to persuade these innocents that what they were intending to do was feasible; when it was the most harebrained, crazy plan of operation he had ever been party to.

'It will be our task to knock out that base so that the Egyptian people can rise against the English oppressors without fear of military intervention. Once Alexandria revolts, so I have been assured by our Egyptian friends, all of Egypt will be up in arms. The Eighth Army's supply lines will be cut to the desert. They will be forced to move large numbers of troops from the front to deal with the revolt. In that moment, Field-Marshal Rommel will launch an all-out attack on the 8th Army's positions and sweep all before him.' He pressed the fingers of his right hand to emphasise his point, as if he were crushing a fly in them. 'The British will be finished. They won't be able to stop running till they reach the Suez Canal – and Egypt will be ours.'

He paused for breath and stared at his men's faces. They were glowing with excitement and he knew what thoughts were flashing through their heads: youthful dreams of glory, leading a popular revolt against the British oppressor to return home to the Reich, laden with medals, with flowers cast at them as they marched through the streets by pretty young girls in Hitler Maiden uniforms. Perhaps even a reception by the *Führer* himself! It would be the summer of 1940 all over again: that heady June of victory when it had seemed Germany had won the war and was well on the way to creating a new and better Europe, freed of the decadence, injustice and inequality of the past.

He forced his own gloomy thoughts to the back of his mind. 'Comrades, I shall be working out the details of our attack on Mustafa Barracks with your officers and NCOs later, but before I dismiss you, I should like to enquire if you have any questions.'

'Yes sir,' the cry went up from a score of enthusiastic throats. '*WHEN? … WHEN DO WE ATTACK?*'

Von Dodenburg looked at their excited faces, eager for some desperate glory, and felt sadness welling up inside him. He swallowed hard.

'On the morning of 24 October, 1942…' He answered, then he could no longer bear to look at them. Almost brutally, he cried 'Dismiss!'

The die had been cast.

SECTION FIVE:

STAB IN THE BACK

'Listen Schulze, I can't risk those boys back there on a half-assed job like this. I need more gen before I attack that barracks.'

Major von Dodenburg to Sergeant-Major Schulze, Alexandria

ONE

Standing with his staff next to his caravan, Montgomery felt the sudden shock of silence. For the first time since he had arrived in the desert, there was absolute silence. Not a gun, not a rifle fired.

It was a beautiful night. The desert was bathed in white moonlight, outlining the hundreds of tanks and trucks waiting for the battle to begin. Here and there a soldier stood next to his vehicle, cigarette cupped carefully in his hand, staring to the front, where the Germans lay waiting for them.

For once in his life Montgomery was nervous. It had taken him nearly twenty-five years of service to get this far in the Army. Now all that effort, all that preparation, all that heartache and self-sacrifice could be destroyed in a flash if this battle went wrong. He had enemies enough in London; they wouldn't give him a second chance. He *must* win at El Alamein!

The minutes ticked by. Nine o'clock passed. Across the way Horrocks came out of his caravan. He seemed his usual happy self. Nine-thirty! There was not much time left. Montgomery said a quick prayer. Ahead of him the men at the vehicles were tossing away their cigarette ends – they glowed like fire-flies in the sand – and were clambering into their cabs.

Suddenly the whole sky to his front blazed with light. For what seemed a long time, there was no sound. From left to right, as far as he could see, the dead-white lights flickered and danced soundlessly. Then the sound of 1,000 guns firing hit him an almost physical blow in the face, so much so that he reeled back, repelled by that tremendous overwhelming noise.

His mood of reverie vanished in a flash. He tried to picture what Stumme at the receiving end of that murderous barrage must be thinking at this moment. He must know now what was coming. How ready was the German commander to tackle him when the barrage ceased and the troops began to move forward into the battle? Could he pull it off?

He turned and walked back to his caravan. His staff followed automatically. Behind him the enemy line began to glow here and there, indicating that a German gun position had been hit and was burning. Montgomery did not look back, although Brigadier Dennis, the commander of 30th Corps' artillery, was crying out loud with passionate enthusiasm, 'Oh, I say – good shooting! ... Bang on, chaps, really bang on!'

Instead he stopped at the door of his caravan and said to his Chief-of-Staff, General Francis de Guigand, 'Freddie, I think I'll turn in now.'

'And the battle?' the burly staff officer asked, a little surprised at his Chief's intention, although he knew Monty of old.

Montgomery's eyes twinkled in the ruddy glare of the barrage. 'The battle, Freddie?' he asked. 'That thing – that thing will take care of itself. Good night.' With that, the General mounted the stairs to his bunk and waiting glass of hot milk, as if he had not a care in the world.

The Battle of El Alamein had begun!

★ ★ ★

Waiting tensely in the doorway of the street in which she had her apartment, Slaughter saw the faint-pink fluttering on the horizon. Jerry must be getting a bashing on the front, he told himself, but he had more important things to concentrate on. Up the street, a flash of blue light broke the blackout. It flicked on and off three times. It was the signal he was waiting for. The SAS troop was in position.

'Come on,' he whispered urgently to the boy.

The boy stuck the goad sharply into the donkey's backside and with a grunt, the awkward brute moved into the alley. The two of them, dressed in the rags of the fellaheen, started to wander down, knocking at each door in turn and bawling out the wares they had to sell.

As Slaughter had anticipated, more curses were directed at them than doors opened. It was the reception he wanted. Up the road the woman's butler would hear the racket and not attempt to activate the alarm system when they came level with her door.

They reached the American woman's house. He nudged the boy; 'Ready?' he whispered urgently out of the side of his mouth.

The boy who had taken to the swift, ruthless murdering of the last few days as if he had been born to it, nodded.

Slaughter stopped in front of the back door and raising his head, bellowed at the top of his voice in best pedlar style.

'Go away!' an irritated voice exclaimed from the kitchen. 'Go away, you black pig!'

Slaughter howled again, praising the cheapness of his wares, which it broke his heart to give away at such prices when he already was a poor man with an ailing wife and six starving children to support. Suddenly his heart leapt. The trick was working. Through the poorly blacked-out door, he could see a chink of light. Then came the sound of heavy boots approaching the door. Slaughter looked at the boy. He was already in position, knife held close to his chest.

There was the rattle of a chain being released. Slaughter increased his wailing. The boy tensed. A bolt was drawn back. The door opened slightly. A yellow light sliced into the blue gloom of the blackout.

'Son of a poxed-up whore, why are you disturbing the peace of honest men –'

The butler's words ended in a thick grunt of pain, as the boy's knife struck him in the chest. The bowl of steaming white beans which he had been eating dropped from his lifeless fingers and shattered on the tiled floor. 'Quick!' Slaughter urged.

The boy jammed his heel into the dying man's guts and the butler dropped with a gasp like the air hissing out of a punctured tyre.

Slaughter whistled shrilly. The SAS men, thick woollen stockings over their boots, ran noiselessly down the street. Within seconds, they were in the back of the house, which was heavy with the smell of spiced cooking.

Hastily the men, strung out in single file, weapons at the ready, moved down the long dark passage which linked the servants' quarters. They emerged into a large round hall, decorated with modernistic paintings and Arab wall rugs. From above there came the sound of several voices.

Slaughter jerked his revolver upwards. 'Remember I want the woman alive,' he ordered.

Pressing themselves into the shadows close to the wall, the SAS men started to mount the winding stairs. Slaughter, bringing, up the rear, licked suddenly dry lips. He must get that woman! There could be no slip up now. She was the last link in the chain. Once he knew what the damned American woman knew, he would have the whole rotten bunch of them by the short and curlies. The great revolution would be over before it had ever begun.

Slaughter started. A door had opened above them. The buzz of voices grew louder. The SAS men halted as one. They pressed themselves deeper into the shadows. Slaughter felt his heart racing madly. If they were spotted now, the woman would have a chance of escape. But luck was on their side. Whoever had opened the door, closed it again without seeing the dozen men biding in the shadows only a handful of yards away.

They made the top of the stairs without any further difficulty. Slaughter nodded to the boy again. He knew perfectly what he was to do. While the SAS men grouped themselves on either side of the door under Slaughter's direction, he posted himself directly in front of it.

'Now,' Slaughter whispered.

The boy knocked three times on the door in the Egyptian servant fashion and without waiting for a call to come in, he opened it and stood there, as if surprised, pushing the door even wider open with the side of his right foot.

'Who the Sam Hill are –' a woman's voice cried in English.

Slaughter did not give her time to finish. 'GO!' he commanded. The desert veterans tumbled through the door, pushing the boy to one side. Inside the little group of young men, some in the uniform of the Egyptian Army, sipping green tea scented with mint, scattered in alarm.

A very dark Captain, who might have been Sudanese, grabbed his .38. The SAS corporal was quicker. His sten chattered, its racket deadened by the silencer. The Captain's shirt flushed with blood and he slammed against the wall, his intestines spilling out, fat, grey and palpitating like a hideous snake.

The sight was enough for the rest of the plotters.

Faces contorted with horror, they raised their hands, while the woman was sick into the brass spittoon.

Slaughter had no mercy. Shoving through the ashen-faced Egyptians, stepping over the Sudanese slumped on the floor, he grabbed hold of her fluffy yellow thatch and dragged her face up from the spittoon. 'Look at me, you bitch!' he commanded hoarsely.

Pomme stared up at the Major, her face deathly pale under the mask of rouge, the vomit wet on her lips. 'Why…why are you so cruel?' she asked thickly.

He slapped her across the face with his free hand. 'I'm asking the questions here, you whore', he roared with simulated rage, knowing that the raddled woman would only respond to brutality.

Pomme stared from Slaughter's face to that of the boy who was watching the Englishman's treatment of the woman with undis-guised admiration and she realized instinctively what the relationship between the two of them was. 'Does it give him a charge too if you belt him before you f –' she began with a trace of her old spirit.

Viciously Slaughter struck her again. Her head slammed to one side. When she turned her head to him once more, there was a thin trickle of blood curling down from her right nostril; and her eyes were full of fear.

Slaughter knew she was ready to talk.

TWO

'Alexandria!'

Schulze grunted in answer to von Dodenburg's announcement.

Behind them in the cover of the wadi, the tired Wotan troops ate their midday meal, their vehicles concealed from any prying British aircraft by the Egyptian Army three-tonners. To their front the green of the Delta was laid out like a carpet. Beyond lay Egypt's second largest city. After two weeks of burning desert, it looked very alluring, with its gleaming white buildings, faintly moving palms and eucalyptus trees, and orderly gardens.

It also looked, to von Dodenburg at least, very frightening. Lying there in the hot sand staring at Alexandria through his glasses he felt himself overcome by a sense of pessimistic foreboding. In spite of the heat of the day, he shivered involuntarily.

'Anything wrong, sir?' Schulze asked.

'Must have been a louse running across my liver,' von Dodenburg answered. He put his binoculars back in their case and rolling over on his back, stared at the men. Soon they would begin painting out the iron crosses on their vehicles for the journey through the city towards the barracks. Mingled as they would be with the Egyptian vehicles, with their crews in the same sort of khaki and stripped of German insignia, they would pass as Egyptian Army troops. Once they reached the objective, they would break out their swastika recognition panels to let the civilians know who was really attacking the British barracks. According to the American woman, the revolutionaries would have a camera man hidden in one of the brothels nearby to make a photographic record of the attack. The photos would appear in every paper in Egypt the next day.

Schulze looked at von Dodenburg uneasily. 'If you'll forgive me saying so, sir, you've got a face like forty days' rain. Problems?'

Von Dodenburg nodded glumly. 'Yes, Schulze there are. All I know of the set-up down there in the city is what I have heard from the woman and the Egyptians, and I am not happy with an op based on second-hand info. I can't risk those boys back there on a half-assed job like this. I need more gen before I attack that barracks.'

'You mean you would like me and that other dum-dum, Matz, to have a look for you, sir,' Schulze said, a grin on his big face.

Von Dodenburg's face remained grim. 'You understand the risks you'll be taking, Schulze,' he said.

'I've been in more dangerous whorehouses, sir,' Schulze said easily. 'Those buck-teethed Tommies'll have to get up early to nab Mrs Schulze's little boy.'

Von Dodenburg laughed with relief. 'All right, you big rogue – and thanks. Good, this is the way I suggest you do it. Get rid of the Wotan armband and your badges of rank. In that khaki you won't look any different from the Tommies themselves. You can use one of the Egyptian trucks to get you into the town without attracting any attention.

'My plan is to move in as soon as it's dark. The blackout should keep most of the civvies off the streets. If we are stopped, the Egyptians can – I hope – talk us out. I intend to attack at midnight.'

Schulze nodded his understanding. 'And where do we fit in, sir?'

'You'll go in an hour before I do. You will recce the area of the barracks. You know what to look for. If you have the least suspicion that things are not what they should be, you will warn me.'

'How, sir?'

Von Dodenburg's eyes twinkled momentarily. He had a shrewd suspicion that it was Schulze who had shared Pomme's bed during her night at the oasis. 'Like this. The American woman has a radio hidden in her apartment – the Egyptian Major will give you a street map and how to get to the place, fourteen Rue de Gaza. If you see anything you don't like, signal me immediately. But remember Schulze, don't take any risks. If the Tommies capture you, they might well take it into their heads to shoot you as a spy.'

Schulze hardly heard the warning. His mind was full of the woman. 'Don't worry about me, sir,' he said gleefully, his eyes gleaming, 'let me just find that ape-shit Matz and get on my way!'

* * *

The two Wotan men in the shabby Egyptian Army three-ton truck reached Alexandria just after dark. It was full moon, and the city was lit by a smooth white light that lay on the buildings like a powdering of frost. The suburban streets were very quiet, as von Dodenburg had predicted they would be, and the few civilians about took no notice of the truck; they had seen enough of them in these last three years of war.

Using the map, Schulze directed Matz at the wheel round the town centre and into the quieter streets of the suburbs where the barracks were.

It was very cold and the sky was rich with the silver glare of the stars. The narrow alleys, no wider than corridors, were completely empty, so utterly so that they had the spookiness of a long abandoned house. Here and there too, he noted that doors had swung open to reveal no light from within the dark wells of houses, as if the population had hurriedly packed a handful of belongings and fled. Even the odd hairless pi-dog, shivering in the gutter, was silent.

Awed by the quietness, Schulze lowered his voice almost to a whisper when he had to give directions. Now he knew that they were only a couple of streets away from Mustafa Barracks. Suddenly he made a decision. 'Matzi, pull up over there – next to that wall.' Grumbling a little, Matz brought the three-tonner to a halt. 'Now what?' he demanded.

By way of an answer, Schulze dropped from the cab and then as an afterthought, reached in to pull out his machine pistol. 'Grab hold of yer pea-shooter,' he commanded, 'and let's get on with it. This place puts years on me.'

In heavy silence they plodded through the deserted streets, keeping to the shadows cast by the high walls, doubling rapidly across the open spots drenched in brilliant moonlight. Schulze felt his hands begin to sweat. Twice he tried to fight off the desire to check whether any one was following them and twice he failed. There was no one. He shuddered violently and told himself not to be a fool.

They passed down another street. Beyond it, Schulze knew from the map, the barracks were situated. Schulze gripped his machine pistol in his sweating hand. 'Matz,' he whispered, 'watch it. The barracks are round the next bend.'

They moved towards the end of the street, noises from the direction of the barracks becoming apparent. At the corner the two of them halted. Cautiously Schulze poked his head round. He gasped with shock.

'What is it, Schulzi?' Matz asked in alarm.

For a moment, Schulze was unable to answer. 'Take a look at that, Matzi,' he whispered.

Matz peered round Schulze's bulk and he too gasped at what he saw there.

Along the walls of the barracks, hastily slung arc lamps glared down, careless of the stringent blackout regulations. In their bright white light, scores of red-faced Tomrnies – many of them elderly and obviously second-line troops, some of them bandaged as if they had just been called hastily from the local military hospital – laboured at their tasks: filling sandbags and erecting walls around the long barrelled guns that were being wheeled into position everywhere in the alley ways and courtyards around the barracks. 'Anti-tank guns,' Schulze cried hoarsely, 'and you know what that means, Matzi?'

'Ay,' Matz said quietly, *'the bastards know Wotan is coming!'*

THREE

'Stop here, Matzi!' Schulze hissed.

The truck, its engine already switched off, came to a halt with only the slightest of noises. For a moment the two Wotan men sat there in the blacked-out cab staring down the long street.

To their right was the bulk of a hotel, but no light came from within. Beyond, the left side of the street was as black as hell. A whole battalion of Tommies could have been hiding there and they would not have been able to see them.

They clambered out and began to walk down to number 14. The sound of their footsteps echoed and re echoed from the high walls on both sides. Schulze and Matz hauled off their desert boots and thrust them into their pockets hastily. They went on, almost having to feel their way through the inky darkness of the shadow. The house they sought was perhaps a matter of fifty metres away now.

Suddenly Matz grabbed Schulze. 'There's somebody up there,' he hissed urgently. 'Look.'

Schulze screwed up his eyes and could just make out the faint glow of a cigarette, and whoever was smoking it was standing outside Number Fourteen.

Schulze's mind raced. Who would be hanging around on a cold city street in pitch darkness at this time of night? he asked himself. He edged his way from the street into a sort of a courtyard. It was too dark to really make out, but Schulze sensed that it was rectangular, hemmed in by a compact mass of silent buildings. From somewhere came the hollow boom of a clock sounding the hour. His lips moving silently, Schulze counted the strokes. Eleven o'clock. The CO would now have begun his move into Alexandria.

'Matzi, I've got a nasty feeling that they've stuck a guard on Madame Pomme's front door. God knows what's going on at her place, but we've got to get in there and warn the CO. Otherwise it'll be murder for the Company. Those poor turds will walk right into the shit.'

'The backway?' Matz suggested hastily.

'Right. Come on, let's see if we can find it in this mess.'

They skirted the buildings of the courtyard. For a few moments they felt their way along a high wall, but it ended in a windowless building, which might have been some sort of storage shed. 'No good,' Schulze cried in exasperation. 'Back!'

They retraced their steps. Schulze tripped and floundered full-length over some stairs. Underneath him he felt something squirming and alive. He got up with a frightened yell. A cat shot over his stockinged feet. Schulze held his breath, but the sound died away with out any reaction. The buildings all around remained silent.

Cautiously they started to mount the stairs, feeling the cold stone through their foot-rags. Reaching upwards Schulze felt what he took to be some sort of wrought iron grille. 'Looks like a balcony, Matzi,' he whispered. 'Let's have a look.'

A thin blue knife of light had slid into the courtyard below. The two NCOs froze. There was a faint hiss of tyres on the cold surface of the yard. It was a man on a bicycle. There was a grunt, which they took to be a man getting off his mount. For a moment there was total silence, then knuckles rapped on glass. A window opened and light flooded the courtyard momentarily and illuminated the man.

There was a brief interchange of words between the cyclist and someone inside, which the two men pressed tight against the balcony wall could not understand. But they did not need to. The cyclist was in British uniform and he had a rifle slung over his shoulder!

The light went out, but the cyclist did not move away immediately. From above they could hear the rasp of a match. Red flame spurted up and the watchers could see the man puff at the cold pipe gripped between his teeth until apparently satisfied he dropped the match and went on his way.

'Christ!' Schulze whispered, 'Madame Pomme has been forced to tell the Tommies what's going on. That's why they're digging in those anti-tank guns at the Barracks. These are guards, waiting for dummies like you to walk right into a nice little trap.' He licked his parched lips and for the first time was fully aware of the magnitude of the problem. 'Shit, the Tommies have really got us by the short and curlies this time!'

Schulze bit his bottom lip desperately, his mind racing crazily. By now the Wotan would be well within the city. Should he attempt to break into Pomme's house, even if it were occupied by the Tommies and fight his way to that radio so that he could warn the CO? Or should he bolt for it and try to stop the CO before he ran into the trap? But which way would they take into the city? He cursed. Naturally he did not know. The only place in which he might be able to warn von Dodenburg was in the street that led to Mustafa Barracks. He made his decision. 'Come on, Matzi, let's get out of here, and back to the Barracks.'

'*Barracks?*'

'I'll explain in the truck. Come on, get yer finger out!' In his haste to get over the rail of the balcony, Matz forgot the flowerpots. His right foot unhooked one. Before he could grab it, it sailed over the balcony and exploded below, with what seemed to the horrified SS men the noise of an 88mm going off.

There was a shout of alarm. And another. Blackout regulations flung to the winds, lights began to click on everywhere. Up above them a window was thrown open. A voice shouted something in Arabic; then, surprisingly, in German. Instinctively Schulze looked up. He caught a glimpse of Pomme, her bruised, bloody figure contorted with horror. Next to her a little man in British uniform – obviously the one who had shouted – was leaning out of the window, his revolver raised.

The Tommy aimed. Next to him, Pomme darted forward, a sudden fury in her eyes. With all her strength, she ripped her nails down the side of the Tommy's face. He screamed with startled pain and staggered back. In his agony he pressed the trigger. Pomme threw up her arms. No sound came from her throat. Schulze caught one last glimpse of her fluffy yellow wig slipping down over the face in absurd pathos and then she disappeared from sight.

Scarlet spurts of flame were beginning to stab the darkness. Schulze ran down the stairs with all speed.

'Into the shadow,' he gasped. Now there were excited angry voices crying all around them in the mess of houses. Wildly the two men looked for some means of escape. The exit to the courtyard was already blocked. 'The hatch!' Matz cried urgently. 'At your feet!'

Schulze saw what he took to be the cover for the chute into which went the carbon for the houses' winter heating system. He grabbed it with both hands and heaved with all his strength.

Nothing happened. The damn thing was jammed!

'Over here,' someone shouted. There was a clatter of heavy boots across the cobbles.

Schulze swore and heaved again. He exerted all his strength. The noise of the running feet was getting ever closer. There was a sucking sound and the hatch gave. Matz swung himself feet first into the chute. The next instant he had disappeared with a slight yelp of surprise. Schulze worked himself into the hole, hanging on to the side with one hand the cover with the other. Somehow he managed to replace it. All light vanished. He let go and started to whizz downwards into the unknown murk…

FOUR

At 11.45 on the night of 24 October 1942, 1st Company, SS Assault Regiment Wotan started to rattle into the sleeping suburbs of Alexandria. The little streets did not remain silent for long. Windows were flung open everywhere and the Egyptians, startled from their sleep by the rusty squeak and clatter of tank tracks, stared out in disbelief at the long column of Mark IVs and halftracks, laden with panzer grenadiers, below.

'*German…German…German…*' the exciting discovery fled from mouth to mouth. '*THE GERMAN LIBERATORS HAVE ARRIVED!*' Suddenly the streets were swamped in Egyptians, wild with delight. Men, women and children rushed directly at the vehicles, flinging themselves on the running boards. A girl in a European dress flung her arms round Sergeant Doerr and kissed him madly. The one-eyed Sergeant was so surprised that he did not even have time to run his hand up her short floral dress as he would have done under normal circumstances. An old man dug a packet of Egyptian cigarettes out of his pocket and tossed them into von Dodenburg's turret. Wine and Egyptian brandy appeared from nowhere. Standing next to a perplexed von Dodenburg, the 'Prof' was hit full in the face by a bunch of roses. Flowers scattered everywhere. In an instant the streets were blocked and von Dodenburg raged as he saw his young troopers submerged by cheering, crying civilians, swept by a torrent of emotional relief and wild joy.

For once in his life, von Dodenburg did not know how to cope with the situation. Assault Regiment Wotan had never been welcomed like this before; even back in the Reich the Armed SS were never really popular. He knew he must not let himself be stalled like this. Hastily he picked up the radio mike.

'Sunray to Sunray One,' he barked above the noise to Seitz who, with the Egyptian Major, was leading the column. 'Do you read me, over.'

'I read you Sunray,' Seitz cried and von Dodenburg could tell from the high-pitched enthusiasm of the young second-lieutenant's voice that he had been infected too by the crowd's wild joy.

'Now simmer down, Sunray One,' von Dodenburg said sharply. 'Break loose from that mob and get on with it. Time is precious. Over and out!'

Von Dodenburg stood fuming with impatience, then he heaved a sight of relief for up ahead in the jammed street, Seitz's troop were gunning their engines with a tremendous roar, sending the crazy civilians scattering out of the way in alarm. Next moment, the lead tank, with Seitz and the Egyptian Major in the turret, pulled away, followed by the rest of the troop.

The 'Prof' balanced himself on the edge of the turret and started to harangue the civilians in their own language. But his efforts were without success. The fact that he spoke Arabic encouraged them to flock around and bombard him with excited questions. In despair he turned to von Dodenburg and raised his hands helplessly. 'They simply won't go away, Major,' he began 'I'm afraid I'm not very good –'

The rest of his words were drowned in a blast of gunfire. Von Dodenburg swung round. The white moonlit sky had flushed an angry red. Next instant, there came the frightening chatter of many machine-guns. Screaming hysterically, their brown faces suddenly blanched with fear, the civilians scattered and headed for cover. In a flash they had disappeared back into their houses.

Von Dodenburg grabbed the mike. 'Here Sunray…here Sunray,' he called urgently. 'Sunray One, do you read me?'

'They've,' Seitz threw all radio procedure to the winds in his horror at whatever was confronting him, 'they've got the whole place…'

The rest of his sentence was drowned by the high-pitched wailing note of another set jamming Seitz's radio. Furiously von Dodenburg twirled his own dials, trying to eradicate the thrumming wail. Suddenly with startling clarity, Seitz's voice came through, high and hysterical with pain. '*My arm…oh God in Heaven…my arm…I can't bear it… They're all dead in here…I can't get out…Please, sir, get me out!*'

The frantic plea for help ended in the sharp clear crack of a revolver fired close by. There was the same eerie thrumming of the set for a moment. Then it, too, stopped as the mike fell out of the dead Seitz's fingers.

Von Dodenburg made a quick decision. 'Driver, advance,' he yelled over the throat mike. As the driver thrust home his gear, he called over the radio, 'Sunray here – to all commanders, prepare for action!'

★ ★ ★

'*Halt, driver!*' von Dodenburg cried frantically, as they swung round the corner into the square in front of Mustafa Barracks. Through the swirling mass of black oily smoke, he could see two of his men. One was advancing with hesitant steps, clutching his ruined stomach with both hands. Through his outspread fingers, a horrified von Dodenburg could see a gory red mess of straggling entrails. Just behind him a man lay in the dust looking stupidly at his legs. Where his boots had been there was pink flesh, thrown into relief by the startling whiteness of the stumps. Next instant their stricken tank exploded, its tracer ammunition zig-zagging wildly into the sky.

Von Dodenburg ducked and felt the Mark IV rock like a ship at sea struck by a tremendous wind. Metal pattered heavily against the turret and the force of the explosion dragged the very air out of his lungs. The men had vanished, as had the thick smoke. He gasped with horror. Ahead of him, concealed a moment ago by the murk, there were the deadly British six-pounder anti-tank guns waiting for fresh victims after the slaughter of Seitz's troop. They had walked into a trap.

Schulze and Matz, wherever they might be at that moment, had failed in their mission after all!

Already the Tommy gunners had spotted him. White tracer started to stich the air as the bren-gunners ranged in. In a moment the first armour-piercing shell would come winging his way and at that range the tanks would not have a chance.

'Driver – reverse!' von Dodenburg shouted in a sudden paroxysm of fear. He pushed the 'Prof' to one side and flung himself behind the 75mm. It was loaded with solid shot, instead of high explosive which would have been more effective against the Tommy gunners. But he had not the time to re-load. He must put the Tommies off their aim by getting in the first shot.

He jerked back the firing lever just as the flustered young driver stalled the engines. The solid shot whizzed through the air and missing the nearest anti tank gun position, blasted a great hole in the masonry of the barracks.

'Great balls of crap!' von Dodenburg yelled in fear and frustration, 'sort those fucking gears out, man! Quick!'

His words were cut short by a fearsome bang. Von Dodenburg gasped as he was drenched with cold water. For a moment he was physically and mentally paralysed. Where had the water come from? A shell must have hit the water jerricans at the back of the tank. The terrible realization almost made his sick with fear. The Tommies had infiltrated men behind him and the rest of the column. He was cut off.

Just as the driver started the engine again, and the Mark IV trembled with life, von Dodenburg pressed the trigger of the machine-gun. Tommy gunners were bowled over in a mess of flailing arms in the nearest gun-pit, sprawling over the sandbags suddenly like broken puppets. But their mates in the next gunpit were still alive and kicking. Von Dodenburg could see them ramming home the deadly shell into the breech of their six-pounder.

Again he pressed the trigger. It chattered frenetically. Like angry red hornets the slugs stitched a glowing pattern through the dust in front of the gunpit. He had missed. The Tommy gunners did not. Like a bat out of hell, the AP shell hissed through the air. It lammed into the turret with an awesome crack. The 'Prof' screamed. Von Dodenburg swung round. Reichert was grovelling on the floor, twisting with pain a dark red stain spreading rapidly across the back of his khaki shirt. 'I have been hit,' he said, pulling himself together, in spite of the tears of pain streaming down his face. 'Not…not too seriously, I trust.'

Von Dodenburg ducked again, as the tank was struck once more. It shuddered violently as if it might overturn. Von Dodenburg jerked furiously at the intercom leads so that the driver was almost strangled, and screamed: '*REVERSE…FOR GOD'S SAKE – REVERSE!*'

The driver thrust home reverse. For a split second the world stood still. Across the blazing square the Tommy gunners were reloading furiously. Then the engines revved and the Mark IV, its metal sides gleaming silver with shell scores, heaved backwards.

Engines revving full out, they swung round the corner into the burning column, right into the path of the two SAS troopers waiting with the PIAT. At that range, the two troopers crouched over their anti-tank weapon could not miss. Their bomb whammed right into the engine cowling. The driver's head flew off like an abandoned football, and von Dodenburg's tank came to an abrupt halt. An instant later there was a whoosh of exploding fuel and it began to burn.

FIVE

'Hellfire,' Matz cursed, as the basement rocked and trembled with the thud of the gunfire, 'Somebody's taking a packet.'

'And you can guess who it is, can't you?' Schulze replied gloomily, as he surveyed the heating system, which seemed to have enough cocks, taps, levers and dials for the control room of a U-boat.

'But what can we do about it, Schulzi?' Matz asked, slumping down wearily on a pile of carbon. 'We'll be lucky if we get out of this in one piece ourselves.'

'You are right there,' Schulze agreed. What could they do to help Wotan, hidden as they were in the middle of an enemy city, hundreds of kilometres away from their own lines? Even if they could get to the CO who was probably fighting for his life in the middle of the square outside the Barracks, what help could they give him? By now the Tommy anti-tank guns must have destroyed all the Company's vehicles. And they did not stand a chance in hell of getting away through the desert the way they had come, on foot and without water. Frustrated and angry, he slammed his foot against the boiler-room controls. There was an asthmatic gurgling, as if liquid had suddenly shot through the convoluted mass of pipes.

'Not only looks like a sub's controls,' Matz commented idly, 'but sounds like one too.'

'That's it' Schulze roared, slapping his hand on his knee.

'That's what?'

'Listen, cloth-ears, isn't Alexandria a port?'

'Yes, I suppose so. But –'

'But nothing,' Schulze interrupted him. 'Listen, this is what I want you to do. Haul your skinny little ass out of here and contact the CO. Now you tell him to break off the action the best he can and make for the port.'

'And then?'

'And then,' Schulze announced, drawing himself up to his full height, 'the CO must ask for Skipper Schulze. I wasn't born on the waterfront for nothing. I'm going to get us a boat!'

★ ★ ★

Outside the port's boom, a British merchantman lay at anchor, lights blazing, while half-naked Egyptian stevedores unloaded its cargo into lighters. Schulze crouching in the shadows, his ears full of the fight going on behind him still, breathed a sigh of relief. That meant the boom was open. There would be nothing to stop them getting out of the harbour, save half the Tommy Mediterranean Fleet, lying at anchor within Alexandria's harbour!

Schulze surveyed the port. It was very crowded. He assumed that the merchantmen were there to unload supplies to support the Allied Army in the desert. But they did not interest him. He was looking for something small and fast, very fast – and he must find it soon. Behind him in the city, the snap and crackle of the battle was beginning to swell to a terrifying crescendo. He did not have much time.

He strained his eyes. In the darkness he could make out the outlines of several navy vessels, looming up faintly through the gloom, with smaller craft flitting about among them. Now and again signal lights winked on and off between the vessels.

Then in a sudden flash of light from a suddenly opened hatch he spotted what he sought: a long, rakish-looking boat, armed with a single light gun. It had been a long time since he had last seen a boat like that back in his native Hamburg when a whole flotilla of them had come sweeping proudly down the Elbe to escort a seasick Führer out to inspect the battleship *Deutschland*. But he recognized it immediately. It was a motor torpedo boat: the fastest craft in any Navy. It would have to be the one.

★ ★ ★

Von Dodenburg crouched with the bleeding 'Prof' behind the smouldering halftrack, dead panzer grenadiers sprawled everywhere in the dust. An instant before the SAS PIAT men had blown up the last of the tanks. Now the handful of bleeding survivors forced into the narrow side-street had nothing to defend themselves with save their own personal weapons – and the British fire was getting heavier by the minute. Soon they would drag up their powerful Vickers machine-guns and slaughter the SS men.

Another shell hit the front wheel of the halftrack. The tyre went up in flames. Next to it, two boxes of ammunition strapped to the side burst into flame too.

'Oh, dear God,' the 'Prof' moaned, holding his wound, 'can we not do anything, Major?'

Von Dodenburg shook his head, his face set in a look of despair. 'Afraid not, Prof. They've got us –'

'Sir.'

A familiar voice broke in.

He swung round. It was Matz, his face blackened with smoke, a thin trickle of blood curling its way down his temple.

'Matz where in the name of hell –' von Dodenburg began, but Matz interrupted him urgently. 'No time to explain, sir. Schulze told me to tell you that you've got to get to the harbour immediately.'

It would be a hell of a job to try to disengage his force with the Tommies so close. Besides both ends of the street were blocked. 'It's going to be a bitch to get out of this, Matz,' he expressed his fears openly. 'They've got us by the short and curlies now, I'm afraid.'

'Never say die, sir,' Matz answered cheerfully, wiping away the blood, before thrusting his hand inside his torn shirt to bring out what looked like a mess of putty. 'This'll do the job, sir.'

'Plastic explosive,' von Dodenburg whispered while the NCO busied himself tearing off a chunk and fashioning it into a small ball.

'Where did you get it?'

'A Tommy who suffered a sudden heart attack,' Matz grinned maliciously, 'at the end of my knife.' He clamped the ball of explosive to the wall behind them and held up the time pencil. 'How long shall we give it, sir?'

Von Dodenburg's eyes lit up. Matz was adopting the old House-to-house fighting technique to their own situation; he would blast a way through one wall and another until they were clear of the trap they found themselves in. 'Give it two minutes, you cunning little shit.'

Ignoring the slugs that started to smack into the wall around him, von Dodenburg rose to his feet and shouted urgently. 'Listen everybody. As soon as you hear my whistle, break off the action and rally to me!' Von Dodenburg gave a shrill blast on his whistle. Firing as they came, the tankers and the panzer grenadiers broke from their cover and began to fall back on the wrecked halftrack. Here and there a man was hit and crumpled to the ground. But their manoeuvre had caught their attackers by surprise and it took them a couple of moments to react. By then the first of the Wotan men were already stumbling through the gap in the wall. Wotan – or what was left of it – was on its way.

SIX

Naked save for his boots, Schulze slipped into the lukewarm water, machine pistol slung round his neck. Before him the motor torpedo boat seemed as big as a battleship now, but he had to take it!

Hardly making a sound, he swam slowly round the bow to the rope ladder, which led to the dinghy. As he swam he could hear above the rattle of fire-fight in the town the soft throb of the torpedo boat's engines. The sound pleased him. The boat was preparing to go to sea. With the beam still open, they might just make it yet.

One by one he mounted the rungs, alert for the slightest sound out of the ordinary. But although he could hear voices and movement on the deck above him, everything remained normal. Cautiously he raised his head above deck level. The rating on sentry duty was facing the quay, with his back turned to the sea. To his right, there was a faint chink of light coming from behind the blackout curtain of the bridge. He hoped the occupant would be the man he was looking for.

Gingerly he heaved himself over the side and started to cross the dark expanse of deck. He had almost reached the bridge when a gruff voice rapped: 'Here, what's this – you the ruddy fairy queen or something?'

Schulze spun round. A big sailor stood there, hands on hips, looking at the naked man in bewilderment.

'Well, cocker,' the sailor demanded. 'Lost your ruddy tongue? What ship are you from, chum? And why you run –'

Schulze dived forward. His heavy shoulder caught the sailor in the chest and his words ended in a surprised gasp as the air was knocked out of him. But to Schulze's surprise, the man did not go down. Instead he recovered and jabbed the outstretched fingers of his right hand into Schulze's face, trying to blind him. Schulze dodged them at the last moment. He grabbed hold of the man, burying his own face in the sailor's chest so that he could not try the blinding trick again and sought the Tommy's brawny neck.

The sailor grunted and brought up his knee. Schulze blocked it with his own knee and winced with pain. The sailor, he told himself grimly, must have learned his dirty tricks in the same waterfront dives as him. Thrusting up his powerful arms, he tried to break Schulze's hold. It was a wrong move. Schulze let go suddenly. The sailor stumbled. Next instant Schulze's tremendous hands wrapped themselves around his neck. Feet astride, eyes bulging with effort, veins standing out on his forehead, Schulze exerted all his strength. The sailor thrashed and gasped, wriggling frantically to break that murderous hold. To no avail. The sailor's struggles grew weaker and weaker, then suddenly his body went limp and he hung there lifeless, held upright only by Schulze's grip. Schulze held on to him for a few moments longer before lowering the dead sailor gently to the deck. 'Poor brave bastard,' he whispered and then after taking a deep breath, he continued towards the bridge.

* * *

The British armoured car skidded to a crazy stop. Three men jumped out and set up the bren gun in a flash. Von Dodenburg ducked. A line of slugs slapped along the wall above his head, spurting yellow flame and sprays of plaster every time they struck. 'Back,' he yelled and retreated the way he had come.

Directly behind them two British snipers were firing out of an upstairs window. Von Dodenburg could see the muzzles of their rifles projecting through the window. 'Come on,' he commanded, knowing they would have to brave the snipers' fire now. Pressed tight against the wall, the escapers edged from doorway to doorway. Slugs bounced off the bricks. Here and there a man yelled with pain as he was struck. Matz was wounded again. He cried out in rage and pain and overcome by a sudden madness, he dashed out into the middle of the Street and raising his Schmeisser, completely ignoring the bullets slapping the cobbles all around him, he fired an angry burst upwards.

The glass shattered like a spider's web. There was a shrill scream and one man came sailing out of the window to smash onto the cartridge-littered cobbles, while the other staggered back, his face red with gore. They ran on.

★ ★ ★

Before he could realize what was happening, Schulze's machine pistol butt slammed into his face and sent the jaunty young skipper sailing against the wall of the bridge. The officer's face blanched. 'What...what...' he attempted to stutter, staring in astonishment at the naked giant who had appeared from nowhere on his bridge.

'*Schnauze!*' Schulze rapped, kicking the door closed behind him and flashing a quick look around the tiny bridge. He had been right. The charts and instruments were scattered across the small conning table, as if the scared young officer who faced him had been just planning a course.

'You are German?' the skipper, who did not look a day over twenty, said, dabbing his bleeding face with the end of his silk muffler.

'No, Father Christmas,' Schulze sneered, relieved all the same that the young skipper seemed to understand his language; it would make his task easier. 'Now listen, no harm will come to you, if you do exactly as I say. If everything works out right, Tommy, you'll be spending a nice holiday in Germany, out of the nasty war for good. So listen.'

Carefully he explained what he intended to do, while listening all the time for any unusual movement from outside. But everything seemed to be normal. As yet no one had discovered the dead seaman's body and raised the alarm. But it would not be long before they did; he knew that.

The young skipper looked at him, his gaze a mixture of fear and complete disbelief. 'You can't…get away with that,' he exclaimed. 'It is impossible. *Unmöglich*…impossible!'

'Then you'd better make it possible,' Schulze snarled and raised his Schmeisser. 'Or you'll be a dead duck. Now come on, let's get cracking…'

* * *

'How far now, Prof?' von Dodenburg gasped and halted for a moment in the cover of a buttress. Behind him the panting survivors, most of them wounded, clattered to a stop, grateful for the rest even though the Tommies were still firing at them.

'Quarter…quarter of a kilometre,' the 'Prof' gasped. 'I think this is the *Kasr El Nil*.'

'Thanks,' von Dodenburg swung round to Matz. 'Now, Corporal, what do you think? Where are we going to find Schulze? With this ship of his.'

Matz shrugged. 'All he said was to tell you to come to the docks. He was going to get Wotan a ship.'

Von Dodenburg breathed out hard. 'Alexandria is a damn big port. That rogue could be in any one of a dozen places.' A slug whined off the bricks just in front of the buttress and reminded him again of the danger they were in. 'All right, come on,' he cried. 'We can't just stand here!'

* * *

'My God, man, don't you realize we've got to kill every last one of them!' Slaughter, his face blackened with gun-smoke and his uniform ripped by bullets, cried angrily.

The harassed infantry lieutenant pointed to the cook and the regimental postman dying in the corner of the shattered wall. 'But my lads have had it, can't you see,' he protested. 'They're base wallahs, not fighting men.'

'The bren carrier,' Slaughter snapped, pointing to the little carrier.

'But my driver has been hit,' the Lieutenant objected.

'Drive it yourself then.'

'I can't,' the lieutenant answered.

'No, because you're yellow – you've got a yellow streak a mile wide down your back,' Slaughter cried in rage and snapped at the boy in Arabic. 'Get in.'

He slid into the driver's compartment. Next to him the boy fondled the mounted bren gun lovingly, his dark eyes shining; he had never seen so much killing as he had this night.

Angrily Slaughter clashed home the gear and let out the clutch. The bren carrier jolted forward. At 30mph it rattled along the Kasr El Nil towards the port. 'Get ready with that gun,' he ordered, as the snap-and-crackle of small-arms fire indicated that they were coming closer to the spot where the Germans were trying to break out of the trap.

The boy beamed at him. 'Never fear effendi,' he replied, 'I will do you honour with it.'

They clattered over the debris of war to where a couple of wounded SAS men lay in the gutter next to a smashed tram car, still firing their weapons at a group of houses, walls bullet-pocked as if with the symptoms of some loathsome disease. Slaughter braked. 'Are they in there?' he asked. One of the SAS men, a bloody gash down the right of his face in which his one eye lay like a pearl, croaked in a hoarse Yorkshire accent 'Ay, that the booggers are.'

Slaughter let out the clutch. The carrier shot forward. The fire from the houses where the Germans were holed up intensified. The boy pressed the butt of the bren into his right shoulder as he had seen the British do. He pressed the trigger. Tracer began to zip towards the houses. Bullets pattered against the carrier's armoured sides. Neither the Major nor the boy flinched. Both were possessed by an all-consuming rage and desire to kill the men who had plagued them for so long. This time they would not escape again.

* * *

As the little armoured carrier rattled past the two snipers who were holding up all further progress to the port nearby, von Dodenburg saw his chance. 'Matz, Meier after me!' he barked.

He vaulted out of the window and doubled forward towards the advancing carrier. The boy saw them at once. He swung the machine-gun round. A flood of tracer headed towards them. Meier skidded to a stop and sank to the cobbles, staring at the bloody hole ripped in his thigh, his liquid eyes full of disbelief.

Von Dodenburg and Matz, the veterans, kept going. Instinctively Matz knew what his CO was going to do. When the two groups of desperate men, were separated by a matter of metres, Matz cried, '*Now sir,*' and fired a burst right at the driver's slit. The bullets whined off the metal crazily. Matz knew that they could not hurt the driver, but they could put him off. Just as von Dodenburg ran up the bren carrier's glacis plate, Slaughter, confused by both the tactics and the bullets, braked hastily, throwing the boy face forward against the metal front. Next moment, von Dodenburg was inside the stalled carrier. The boy, his face covered with blood, squirmed round in the tight compartment to face this unexpected enemy. Von Dodenburg did not give him a chance. Balancing on the side of the carrier, he aimed a tremendous kick at the boy's head. The Blue Veil howled with pain, and red and blue lights exploded in front of his eyes and he slumped in his seat stunned.

'You bastard – you German bastard!' Slaughter screamed as he saw his beloved boy fall back. With surprising speed he sprang from his seat and rose to grapple with the man towering above him.

Matz squeezed the trigger of his Schmeisser. Slaughter howled with unbearable anger as the burst ripped his back wide open. Grabbing the air, trying to keep his balance as if he were climbing the rungs of an invisible ladder, he crashed over the side.

Von Dodenburg grabbed the dazed boy by the scruff of his neck and flung him out after his lover. Sobbing blindly, the boy cradled the dead man's head in his lap, stroking the suddenly still face with his brown hand. Major von Dodenburg slipped into the driver's seat and re-started the engine. Matz sprang over the side next to him. Now the survivors began to stream out of the houses behind the cover of the bren. Over the roar of the engine, von Dodenburg yelled: 'Follow me!'

In typical panzer grenadier form, the troopers covered by the firing carrier, advanced and swept by the dead bodies of the two

SAS men, leaving behind the sobbing boy and the dead Major who had saved the day for the man who was soon to be called the 'Victor of El Alamein'.

★ ★ ★

Doubling all-out with the last of their strength, the Wotan troopers ran onto the quay behind the carrier. Tracer was still coming at them from the confused mass of sheds. But most of it was wild and the troopers were too eager to get away from the Alexandria death-trap to worry about it.

Von Dodenburg halted. There were ships everywhere, many of them with their lights blazing. Some of them were merchantmen, but most grey warships. Even if Schulze had pulled off the impossible task of seizing a ship single-handed, how could he hope to get it out of Britain's chief naval base in the Mediterranean, with so many enemy ships present?

'Which way, sir?' Matz yelled.

'If I only knew,' von Dodenburg groaned. Behind them there came the sound of machine-gun fire from one of the sheds. Sergeant Doerr cursed and flung his last stick grenade. There was a thick crump and the firing died away. But it was followed by the sound of running feet.

'This way,' von Dodenburg ordered. Obviously the whole harbour was beginning to wake up to their presence. In minutes the naval base would be roused. He swung the carrier's wheel and clattered down the quay to the right, with the men doubling desperately after it, slugs hitting the concrete or whining off the corrugated iron sheds.

Von Dodenburg felt himself covercome by despair.

Ship after ship flashed by, with their alarmed crews turning on the lights and yelling in anger and surprise at the sight of Germans in their midst. '*Come on; Schulze for Chrissake, come on,*' he called to himself frantically like a frightened child after a nightmare, wishing morning and the light to come again.

The howl of a ship's siren drowned even the growing volume of small-arms fire. 'Oh, shit. What now?' Matz cried above the racket.

'Where's it coming from?' von Dodenburg demanded.

'Over there,' Matz answered, pointing hastily at a Royal Navy torpedo boat.

Von Dodenburg cocked his head to one side, while the panting exhausted troopers clustered behind the carrier for protection…'Can you make it out, Matz?'

Matz's face set in a look of absolute astonishment. 'It's morse… somebody using the hooter for a morse signal.'

'Yes.' Von Dodenburg's eyes glowed with sudden hope. 'Listen to it! W…O…T… *It's Schulze. Come on!*'

The ship was signalling WOTAN.

They doubled towards it, its mighty engines already throbbing, its deck shuddering, like a lean whippet anxious to be let off the leash.

* * *

Schulze watched them come. He pressed his Schmeisser into the pale, but defiant captain's back. 'All right, skipper, get your beautiful sailor boys ready to cast off,' he ordered.

'You swine, you can't –' His protest ended with a yelp of pain, as Schulze poked the muzzle hard into his back.

'I can do anything, Captain,' Schulze said cheerfully, as the Wotan men started to spring across the gap between the trembling boat and the quay. 'I'm the admiral of this particular fleet.'

The young officer spoke into the mike. 'Cast off,' he said, forcing out each word through gritted teeth.

Just as the deckmen flung off the last hawser and the boat began to move out at an ever increasing speed, von Dodenburg took a mighty leap forward and landed on the deck in a heap. 'Good for you, sir!' Schulze exclaimed in delight and shoved the captain's tense back. 'All right, Nelson, full speed ahead!'

* * *

They had almost reached the boom when an echoing voice from the shore demanded: 'What the devil do you think you are playing at, sir?'

'This is it!' von Dodenburg standing at Schulze's side in the heaving bridge tensed.

'I said, sir, what are you doing?' the impersonal voice over the loud-hailer repeated. 'Heave to – or we will fire.'

'All right, Nelson,' Schulze said with more cheerfulness than he felt, as the great shore batteries of 12-inch guns started to swing round in their direction. 'Here's where you win the Iron Cross – Third Class. Hit the gas!'

This time the young skipper needed no urging. He and his crew would go down with the Jerries too if they were hit now. All their lives were in his hands. He opened the throttle full blast. The two Germans caught themselves just in time. The long sharp prow rose right out of the water. At thirty knots an hour, with the boat hitting each wave as if it were a solid brick wall, it shot out into the sea just as the inferno broke loose.

Balls of fire were flung across the chasm of water. Tracer shells spat and ricocheted, dragging a blazing white light behind them over the sea. It was a vast impressive picture of frustrated fury, immense, volcanic and spectacular, like the anger of the gods.

But it was too late. They had gone…

ENVOI

ENVOI

'Oh, bloody! Bloody! Bloody!
All bloody fleas, no bloody beer
No bloody booze since we've been here
Oh bloody! Bloody! Bloody…'

The crazy Australian General prisoner, tied to one of the escape transport's stanchions, was singing with a mad grin on his brown face.

Von Dodenburg, standing next to the 'Prof' at the railing, tried to ignore the dreadful noise and focused his binoculars on the far end of the beach, which was swamped with troops. The *Afrikakorps* was fleeing Africa, or at least some of it was: the generals, Rommel in the lead, specialists and the survivors of Assault Battalion Wotan. Von Dodenburg swept his glasses around the beach and thought he would never forget this tragedy; the sight would be etched on his memory forever.

Everywhere lines of weary men were staggering to the boats, ignoring the shell bursts of the Allied armies which were in the hills beyond, with the foremost ranks shoulder-deep in the water, pleading piteously to be taken aboard.

British planes came zooming in at mast-height, machine-guns chattering. Men sank beneath the waves everywhere and the transports' anti-aircraft guns thudded in a vain attempt to fight the Spitfires off. At the stanchion the Australian General began his crazy dirge once more:

'Oh, bloody! Bloody! Bloody!
Air raids all day and bloody night
They give us a bloody fright.
Oh bloody…Bloody…'

The squadron of Spitfires roared in for one more sortie and then they were off to refuel before coming back to wreak more havoc, soaring high into the brilliant sky. The 'Prof' replaced his new stainless steel false teeth which he kept in his helmet in moments of danger. 'It's about time we went, Major, don't you think?' he said.

'Time indeed,' von Dodenburg agreed, focusing his glasses on the cautious figures who were coming down from the hills now. He was right. They were Tommies. Against the yellow clouds of dust, they were sharply silhouetted in their pudding-basin helmets as they advanced on the Germans. Von Dodenburg's heart ached as he saw the men in the familiar peaked-caps of the *Afrikakorps* being shepherded into disconsolate groups to be led off to the Tommies' prison cages. The Desert Fox's great dream of the conquest of Africa was over. He took the 'Prof's' arm. He wanted to see no more. 'Come on, Prof, let's get below. We'll be sailing in a minute. I've had enough of North Africa.'

At the stanchion, the tied prisoner sang:

'Best bloody place is a bloody bed
With blanket over bloody head.
And then they think you're bloody dead.
Oh bloody! Bloody! Bloody! …'

* * *

At the gangplank, Schulze, again elevated to the temporary rank of full colonel with the aid of the epaulettes hastily fixed to his shoulders, looked down at the lighter full of *Afrikakorps* staff officers, rummaging around in their kit wondering what they should take with them for the trip to Italy. Once the great men had been accustomed to settling the lives and fates of thousands of men with a snap decision; now they could not make their minds up which one of their bulging cases to take with them on board.

'Colonel' Schulze gazed down at them in contempt, while Matz stared at the rich pickings with rapacious, greedy little eyes. '*Meine Herren!*' Schulze drawled at last in his best Prussian Guardee's voice, 'would you please get your digits out! We sail in exactly five minutes – or we get sunk one minute later. One case per officer, *please*. Now make it snappy!'

The threat worked. In one minute flat the staff officers were clambering up the rope ladder and hurrying below with their single cases, leaving an evilly grinning Matz to collect their leavings.

'Well?' Schulze demanded when Matz had swung himself up on board again, the loot clutched to his skinny chest.

'Four chests of cigars, two bottles of wine and a bottle of Algerian brandy – and two dirty books.'

'Excellent, excellent, my boy,' Schulze boomed in his officer's voice. 'I'm beginning to like retreats – you eat and drink better and meet a more interesting type of individual, what.'

'Up yours!' Matz said by way of an answer.

Five minutes later as they lounged in one of the lifeboats, 'rented' from an obliging deck officer for one case of cigars, the transport finally started to pull out from the Algerian bay, its siren shrieking.

Schulze looked reflectively at the African coast. A gleam came and went in his bright-blue eyes. It might have been one of rage, or of relief. It would have been hard for the observer to discover.

Schulze raised one large buttock and gave one of his lazy, musical farts, celebrated in sergeants' messes throughout Occupied Europe. He lifted his mug of cognac in toast as the coast faded into the smoke of battle, and called with heart-felt relief: '*AUF WIEDERSEHEN AFRIKA...*'